ELLOWYN BEIMLER

Undeath on the High Seas

First published by Nerdworthy 2024

This novel is entirely a work of fiction. The names, characters and incidents portrayed in it are the work of the author's imagination. Any resemblance to actual persons, living or dead, events or localities is entirely coincidental.

Ellowyn Beimler asserts the moral right to be identified as the author of this work.

First edition

ISBN (paperback): 979-8-9868717-6-9
ISBN (hardcover): 979-8-9868717-7-6

Cover art by Mahlia Mesa

This book was professionally typeset on Reedsy.
Find out more at reedsy.com

This book is for everyone who's supported me on my journey.

And for every person who got excited at the mere mention of a zombie apocalypse on a cruise ship.

Thank you to all my friends who made this happen, my parents for supporting me, and Mouse and Mars for reminding me to take breaks.

Old and young, we are all on our last cruise.

Robert Louis Stevenson

Contents

1

Chapter 1

They ended their time in Southeast Alaska's Inside Passage with patches of clouds intermittently covering the sun. Fate had been smiling on them for the last couple of days. The forecast had predicted a cold rain, but all the sleepy little towns were graced with clear skies instead of the usual "liquid sunshine."

As the ship slowly made its way out of the inside passage, a gentle breeze ruffled Penelope's hair, bringing the crisp, soothing scent of the ocean. The sun is perfectly positioned, warming her legs without blinding her, and the clear blue sky and untamed green forests are reflected on a deep, dark sea. The distant roar of the ship covers all other sounds, and Penelope is just getting into the first book in her bag when Teagan and Courtney stop by.

Courtney slams the sliding glass balcony door open, something Penelope hadn't thought possible, and yells, "Found her!"

Penelope jumps hard enough at the interruption that she nearly throws her book. Maybe she should have saved the horror novel for later.

Or at least for when her friends weren't scaring the bejesus out of her.

Teagan pops her head out after Courtney. For once, her chestnut hair is loose from its usual severe, slicked-back bun. As usual, she's distracted by her ancient phone, probably texting her boyfriend as she says, "Hey! Should have figured you'd be hiding away."

"Well," Penelope begins, tucking her feet under her chair. She doesn't really have an excuse—she was hiding. "I just wanted to avoid the crowds."

"Courtney wants to explore the ship, maybe take some aesthetic pics. Wanna join?" Teagan asks before Courtney can.

Penelope gets more comfortable and smiles, "No thanks, I finally got comfortable."

"But it's gonna be fun!" Courtney whines, giving Penelope puppy dog eyes. Unfortunately for her, it's much less effective now than in elementary school, when she'd had the big doe eyes and dark curly pigtails to match. "We can even see the boring parts of the ship you'll like!"

"I find reading just a liiiittle more comfortable than posing for you forever." Penelope's already done three shoots for Courtney and wasn't feeling up to more.

Courtney pouts, crossing her arms over her stark white crop top. She looks like she's going to argue more, but Teagan cuts her off.

"Okay, we'll see you at dinner then." Teagan looks up from her phone long enough to smile and wave, braces unable to diminish her pearly whites. As they leave, she shouts, "Enjoy your book!"

Penelope half-salutes, watching through the balcony door as they grab another bag—likely full of props and clothes—and head off. Penelope knows they'll probably take way too many pictures that Courtney will edit and then pass out to the rest.

Presumably, to post on their own socials.

Even if she were into that lifestyle, Penelope will wait to post anything. She's heard one too many stories of people coming home to find that they'd been robbed. Even though she has roommates—and she's probably more at risk of them stealing her stuff—she'd prefer to avoid that.

Penelope settles in again and relaxes into her book, letting her dark hair loose around her shoulders to help keep the cool breeze at bay.

She's glad they're all still friends, but a vacation is supposed to be relaxing.

Even if they did go to see stuff like the engines or the ship's bridge, she'd be the only one enjoying it. Though, they would get some cool pictures if they were allowed to take them.

... — — — ... ... — — — ... ... — — — ...

After a while, Penelope notices the slight catch in her throat and thinks about getting a drink, only to be startled again by the door to the room slamming open.

"You're never gonna believe it!" Melissa shouts as she crashes into the room, shattering Penelope's peace again.

Penelope hopes Melissa will get the message by burying her face in her book. However, she continues to chatter, obviously missing the fact that Penelope isn't paying attention. Resigning herself to her fate, Penelope chooses to actually pay attention to her friend.

Melissa's tousled blonde hair bounces as she flits around the room, gushing the guy she met. "-He's so sweet and such a good listener! And I was telling him about how I'm looking for a job-"

Penelope listens to her besotted friend as Melissa puts on clean clothes and chatters away. She's wearing the same sundress she wore last night when she went to "watch a movie." Other than her hair being a bit of a mess, she looks happy.

Glowing, really.

Maybe Teagan's wedding isn't the only one we'll be going to soon, Penelope thinks to herself, nodding as Melissa keeps talking.

"-He says that there's a school district near him looking for art teachers, and you know I minored in that, but I was thinking it might be a good idea to apply there anyway-"

She seriously doubted it would actually happen. Though it is fun to see how Melissa acts, bouncing and moving through the cabin with vitality, whenever she meets someone new, she always plans their whole lives together immediately. She would make a decent life coach if her dreams didn't bounce around as much as she was now. But she was happy and could be as "in love" as she wanted as long as she could hold down a job.

"-And if I do get a job there, maybe having a friend there can help me get settled. I mean, he's gotta know all the best places to hang out and-"

Penelope smiles and nods as her friend talks. Even though the interruptions are irritating, the rest of the cation will be perfect for reading. Besides, this will be the last time she sees her friends for a long, long while. She'd only come on this trip because of the lull between her summer job ending and her big new fancy job starting.

"-He's just so nice, and he constantly talks up his friends. Can you just imagine him doing the same about me? I mean, not that I expect him to, but he's so outgoing and just-"

She tries to enjoy it while she can. Usually, Melissa gets too into whatever she's working on to remember to tell the others about her current boy toys, often leaving them confused when she shares news without updates in between.

And while Brody is apparently the best man ever, Penelope is sure he's just another in a long line of them. However, he probably will hold a special place in Melissa's heart just by virtue of being her first love at sea.

"-I'm probably just getting ahead of myself again." Melissa stops, looking over at Penelope.

Penelope freezes, her muscles tensing. Should she say something? What? She hadn't been listening, and that didn't sound like a question.

She tries to cover up her panic, but Melissa shrugs before she can say anything.

"Eh, at worst, I have a job, right? So Brody lives in-"

Crisis averted.

Penelope allows herself to go back to thinking. She's really enjoying Alaska. A beautiful cruise ship with stunning sights, friendly people, and lots of sun. Not to mention tons of time with her friends. Kodiak was gorgeous, just like all of Southeast Alaska. There were undoubtedly upsides to living in this part of the world, friendly people aside. Maybe she can get a job traveling in this part of the world. There is always a need for tech people, and stuff on the cruises probably needs fixing.

Who would I need to talk to about that? She wonders.

"-But he probably knows about some places that might be cheap or easy to rent, right? Not that I need him to help me find a place. I can do it on my own, but it'd be nice to have someone to help with all the bills. I wouldn't ask Brody to-"

Although Information and Technology wasn't Penelope's first choice, it was a good path, and she'd make decent money. The biggest downside she's noticed is that everyone goes to her when they have computer issues.

Her mom disapproved, but her mom had met her dad before leaving college and thought a Mrs degree was the most important one a woman could have. It doesn't mean that Penelope wants to do the same.

She just needs her mom to stop setting up blind dates for her without any warning. Well, the one with Frakenlin hadn't been the worst blind date, except that she was a woman, and that really wasn't what Franklin was looking for in a partner.

She should call him when she gets home; if nothing else, he was fun to talk to.

"Do you think I should invite Brody to dinner?" Melissa asks her, and Penelope thinks for a moment.

She taps her lip as she thinks. It's not something she's crazy about, but she's pretty sure they're not allowed to have guests. She isn't going to tell Melissa that, though.

"I thought we were going to spend some time together. You know, like we'd planned?" Penelope does her best to avoid wincing. She can admit it came out a little... well, a lot worse than she'd planned. "You're spending so much time with this guy. Let's have a girl dinner, and you can introduce us later."

"You know what? You're so right. And I am all over that." Melissa says, coming over and giving Penelope a quick squeeze, briefly enveloping her in a cloud of sweet perfume before returning inside.

Penelope sighs with relief, then notices Melissa packing an extra change of clothes. "Or are you just planning to not see us until tomorrow if we won't have dinner with him?"

Melissa blushes, a pretty thing influencers wish they could replicate. "I need them for dinner, obviously! I'm not just going to dip on you guys."

Penelope is pretty sure they both damn well know that the clothes are for her next overnight stay with Brody. She smiles at her anyway. "Go have fun, just message one of us if you're not coming so we know not to wait around."

Melissa beams and calls, "Okay-love-you-bye!"

Even though she's mostly out the door, Penelope calls back, "I do want to meet that boy of yours! Eventually!"

2

Chapter 2

Penelope's dinner alarm startles her next, the late hour sneaking up on her. She's been judging by the sun, which looked like it was just touching the horizon. She thought that she still had plenty of time.

However, her phone alarm keeps blaring, confirming the late hour—almost eight—and she hasn't eaten since lunch.

Unsurprisingly, to Penelope, she's the first to arrive. It's still too early for her to sit at their table, but that's why she brought her book. She pauses outside the dining room to give herself a once-over in the fancy gold vine-bordered mirror.

The dining room rules include that everyone is dressed up, so Penelope even took her time getting ready. A simple, loose plum peasant blouse tucked into her black skirt was a timeless combination with some bangles borrowed from Courtney. Courtney probably won't mind. Most likely. Skirts were always so much easier than pants of any kind; she never had to worry if they'd fit her hips and thighs and waist. As long as they fit her waist they'd fit her hips and thighs, too. Her corset belt emphasizes her waist and gives her a distinguished outline if she says so herself.

Given how early she was running, she'd even taken the time to tease her hair out, emphasizing her natural volume.

But here she was, still wishing she'd taken more time with it.

Teagan and Courtney pop up a little while later, talking about their day. Their bags looked much less neatly packed, and they were both in nicer outfits than they'd left in.

"-You wouldn't think getting there would be so hard! Who could have guessed they'd be closed?" Courtney said as they turned the corner.

"Well, it's not like they didn't have it posted, Court." Teagan notices her first, "Oh, there's Penelope! I told you she'd probably beat us here."

"Hey guys!"

"Omg, Pen, you would not BELIEVE some of the pictures we got. The views were incredible!" Courtney exclaims as she drops onto the cushioned bench next to Penelope. Crossing her legs to avoid another miniskirt mishap, she reaches into her bag, pulls out her camera, and gestures wildly with her other hand.

They give Penelope a rundown of the different places they've visited, show her pictures, and tell her about the people they've bumped into. It did look like they were having fun in the pictures, even with Teagan bemoaning how hard it was to get nice photos. She also complains about how many they messed up. And Penelope was absolutely right about the bag of props, all of which look well used.

As they scroll through the images, Courtney lets out a sigh.

"It was so hard getting good lighting in some of these places. The golden hour doesn't start until right when we have to leave for dinner, and while that makes exploring the ship easier, it doesn't help with getting those 'perfect vacation photos.'" She flops against the wall, flipping through her pictures. "Is it really too much to ask for some sunset photos?"

"Apparently. Maybe that just means we'll need to travel together again. Somewhere, the sunset isn't in the middle of the night." Teagan tells her.

Penelope hums, "Or maybe it's a sign we must stay up tonight? Get some of those 'nightlife' photos?"

She doesn't want to do that, but it's worth it for how Courtney squeals and hugs her.

Penelope notices Melissa—no extra guest in sight—saving her from having to talk more about photography. They're just in time for dinner.

Covering her sigh of relief with a stretch, Penelope asks, "Did you get anything cool while we were in port? You were looking for a magnet or something, right?"

The others tell their tale of woe. Apparently, this is the plight of late-season cruises. All the local businesses are running out of everything, and no one's reordering because it's the end of the season.

Their usual dinner group sits with them—a family with small children taking up the remaining seats—which doesn't really make it a girls' night. Still, it's better than watching Melissa fawn over her new boy toy, Brody.

Especially as they're only allowed one glass of wine with dinner.

The parents look frazzled, the bags under their eyes looking deeper than before.

Penelope thought this was supposed to be an easier way to travel but no matter where you took your kids, it would be exhausting. At least it would make the routine of home more appealing.

When the food arrives, Courtney stops the group and says, "Wait! I want to take pictures of everyone's food."

Penelope sighs, pushing her food toward her friend while wishing she had more wine.

"You know there's going to be plenty of stuff to take pictures of, Court," Melissa says with a little smile. "You don't have to do it every meal."

"I know, I know. I just want everyone to see how awesome this cruise is." At least Courtney is taking these pictures on her phone. The quality won't be as good as her camera, but they'd kept her from doing that from day one. No one wanted to be that table.

Even if they still were at that table.

The parents were busy trying to keep their kids from throwing their food to comment on the picture taking. They'd done it the first night when the kids were still well-behaved and they had a leg to stand on. Privately, Penelope laughed, thinking they deserved it for being so pretentious when they'd first met.

For Courtney, taking her photos was just another way of enjoying their trip, and the couple didn't need to bash it because they didn't understand it.

Penelope didn't want to ruin Courtney's fun but would rather eat her food while it was still hot. Mainly because it was another fish course. The last one had been rubbery when she'd gotten to eat after it sat for far too long.

Mentally shrugging, Penelope distracts herself by looking around. The room is full of other people, other groups traveling on the nearly last ship of the season. Not a lot of families, but also not many people around her age. Mostly elderly folks or middle-aged couples clearly trying to reignite the spark. The room is low-key fancy, with high ceilings, dark draping cloth around the perimeter, and white tablecloths everywhere.

But looking around the room gets boring quick, so she asks the kids beside her if they've had fun. Of course, they have opinions on everything. They told her about the lumberjack show in Ketchikan, one of the first ports the ship had stopped in. The littlest one apparently even got a chair out of the whole deal. Penelope sees the parents sigh; it would probably be a hassle to transport.

Eventually, Courtney slides her food back after taking a million photos.

It's another salmon dish, probably farmed based on all the stickers on the cars in all the little towns. It is pretty good, if a little bland, and she could taste a hint of ranch. It was still enjoyable even though it had probably cooled well past its prime.

A loud clatter from across the room catches the attention of the room. The sounds of dinner quiet immediately as people look at the woman now standing, her black dress glittering in the light like a sea of stars.

She slams her fists into the table, once, twice, again. Her long, loose hair bounces as she moves.

Penelope watches, eyebrows trying to become one with her hairline, as the woman screeches at her table.

Her voice drops as a man near her stands, hands up, placating. Still, she punches her dinner companion anyway before storming off.

The man drops, blood covering his white shirt immediately, and before anyone can react, a couple servers appear, fussing over the man with a first aid kit and calling security.

They watch for a moment. Penelope wonders what was said and why the woman freaked out.

"Oh! You know what we should do after dinner?" Courtney asks. The silence probably getting to her. Without waiting for a response, she continues, "I was looking it up earlier, and there's all kinds of stuff we can do in the evenings that we haven't done yet. There are shows, dancing, and a casino! We should all go to the casino."

It takes her a moment to respond; Penelope is sure that's a bad idea. "I don't know. I mean, the house always wins."

"Well, yeah, but the point of a casino isn't to win money; it's to have fun. At worst, you break even and have a good time." Teagan tells her, gesturing at her with a tiny potato.

"I think I'm going to cite the old adage of 'A fool and his money are soon parted.'" Penelope says, finishing off her own potatoes.

"It's not like we're paying for most of this trip. We can afford to lose a little money." Teagan points out. "Also, you can't keep going to bed early. You've gotta explore a little. It'll be good for you to see some of the sights. And your books will still be there when you're done. We'll be at sea for a week; you can read them then."

"If you're trying to avoid losing all your money-" The dad at the table adds. Penelope's completely forgotten his name. "-when you're gambling, you gotta play blackjack; the odds are pretty much even there, and you've got a better chance of at least winning your money back."

"See? You can play blackjack!" Courtney pleads, puppy eyes back again.

"Aw, we should all go. It'll be something we can all enjoy." Melissa tells her. After a short pause, she adds, "Mostly."

"Traitor." Penelope mutters before saying louder, "Fine, we can go. I think we're even all dressed up for it."

The others cheer, and Penelope admits, "I don't think I've gone to that part of the ship before. Or even near it, actually."

"Wonderful!" Melissa says, "Oh, and it'll be a perfect time for you guys to meet Brody!"

Ah, just what she'd been trying to avoid. Penelope is uncomfortable with that, but she's willing to try. Well, try to have fun and not judge Brody too much.

But it'll be nice to spend more time with her friends.

Even if it is in a loud, smelly casino that will probably have too many people, too much alcohol, and way too much noise.

"This is great!" Courtney tells the others, "Let's get some pictures of all of us at dinner, too!"

Flagging down one of the servers, she asks if he'd take their picture, and Penelope tries to grin more than grimace.

Sure, she was hoping to get some alone time, and she'll want to hide away even more after this, but this is what she does for friendship.

Like possibly losing all her money at a casino.

Ugh.

3

Chapter 3

"You know, I'm related to Elizabeth Peratrovich." This guy, Neil— Brody's friend—was not getting the hint. Neil's been trying to chat Penelope up since Melissa introduced them.

"Who?" Penelope asks without looking. She knows who Elizabeth Peratrovich was and why she's important to the area. She just didn't think that a lady that cool would be all that impressed with being related to such a failure of a fuckboy.

Unfortunately for her, he just keeps talking. And inching closer.

"Yeah, it's actually really interesting; I'm related to so many of the big families around here." Neil drones on, missing that Penelope just isn't interested. At all. Even though she's melting into the table more and more as the man seems to suck her will to live right out of her. Explains why Melissa looked deflated when introducing the other man after Brody's bubbly introduction.

It was more than his off-putting demeanor; he wasn't terribly attractive. Or interesting. And he somewhat reminded her of a hobbit, maybe one of the sackville-baggins. Like he might try to steal her mother's good silverware if she took her eyes off him for too long. Not in a necessarily threatening way. Just... generally unpleasant to be around.

"Wow, " she says flatly in response to his continued blabbering. Stretching her neck, Penelope tries to subtly flag her friends, but they're not paying attention, and she can't see where Courtney has disappeared to.

Once she'd introduced Brody and his friends—unfortunately also including Neil—they'd only stuck around for a drink.

Leaving Penelope alone to deal with Neil.

And his hot, wet breath kept fanning over her shoulder where her shirt had slipped down, never mind her attempts to keep it back up. And he kept leaning into her, moist heat radiating off him like a sauna.

Penelope never liked saunas.

Despite the lack of distance, she can't even call out to her friends between the slot machines' constant, jarring noise and the thrum of people in the room. It's nearly impossible to hear anyone if they aren't beside you. It's definitely not Penelope's idea of a good time. The press of people was too hot, too humid, too much bad, boozy breath. And all her friends have abandoned her.

After their initial drink—and Courtney taking selfies with Penelope and their other friends—they'd gone to a couple of the different tables. There were plenty of options. Courtney wanted to play craps, which was off to the side, while the rest of Penelope's friends remained nearby. Teagan, Melissa, and Brody were at the table next to her, playing poker or something that looked like it from here. They were having fun, Melissa bouncing around, no poker face to speak of, sitting out while Teagan and Brody barter with their substantial piles of chips.

And Neil was following her.

She'd moved from the group and the more intensive gambling, claiming she'd rather not steal from her own friends but really moving away from Neil. Unfortunately, he didn't seem to notice she'd moved tables twice to get away from him.

A sea of people shouldn't be that hard to disappear into; people talking, laughing, drinking, moving, and dancing like they were. The low lights leave the room in shadow except for the game tables and bar. She should be able to slip away. But he's managing to track her, and she's given up on avoiding his attention if she stays in the room.

Blackjack was her choice. Their dinner companion had been right; it was the best odds in the house. But it left entirely too much time for Neil to talk to her. At least she was making her money back with interest, though the time certainly felt wasted having to listen to Neil.

She's nearly memorized the feel of the table, the softer velvet texture of the fabric of the main portion of the table, and the tacky feel of the wood she's leaning against. It was the only thing saving her from Neil's drone and the buzz of people all around her.

Worst of all, the dealer didn't even try to send him away. Probably because—by her count—he was on a hell of a losing streak and down a couple hundred. He wasn't even really playing the game; she, on the other hand, had made enough to cover everything she'd bought on this trip. Really, it's only a matter of time till she gets in trouble for card counting or something.

Penelope bets high and decides to play another round, trying to tune Neil out.

Tuning him is harder than she thought, and even though she's barely responding, he just keeps talking.

Despite her friends' barely there teasing, she didn't see anything exciting about him. Maybe that was why she was introduced to him, and she'd never been the kind of person to have a "vacation fling."

The dealer deals the cards, but Penelope is distracted by the brawl on the other side of the room. Two men have started whaling on each other as other people try to pull them apart.

More people were joining in, beating the shit out of each other, and over what?

Penelope can't tell from here, but she doesn't want to stick around to find out or wait for security to show up. She gathers her winnings—not a lot, but enough to make it worth being here.

Seriously, where was security?

She hesitates before dropping some chips for the dealer—she didn't know if he'd get to keep them—and gets up.

"Hey, hey! Leaving already? Let me walk back to your room. I'm sure Melissa and Brody are living it up in mine right now." Neil jokes, maybe jokes. The upturn of his lip looks more like a sneer than a smile, "And I'm sure the neighbors won't mind as much if someone like you were making all the noise."

Penelope decides she desperately wants to be as far away from this irritating little man as she can. Maybe even in another hemisphere.

"I'm good-" Penelope plasters on a smile, "-just need some air. After winning a few times, I-"

"Well, then, I'll wait for you here! Just don't leave me waiting long, alright?" Penelope nearly gags, but she smiles tightly and leaves. She's pretty sure the dealer is wincing with her.

She cashes out, getting real cash—very nice, she'd been concerned it would be "cruise credit" or something—and leaves the casino entirely.

I didn't like that at all. No, thank you. Penelope shivers, thinking about having to deal with Neil again. Staying in her room sounded like a much better alternative to ever dealing with that guy again.

And if she stayed in her room, she'd be able to deep dive into her new books.

Someone Penelope talked to was saying there might be the northern lights. She thought that was a winter thing, but maybe they'd get lucky. It's as good a reason as any for Penelope to go up to the uppermost deck. Though, really, she's hoping to get some fresh air and maybe stargaze.

The air has a surprising nip, and the skirt she chose for dinner isn't warm enough for outside at this hour, especially not with the wind whipping at her.

Penelope shivers a bit, though not at the cold. Her mind again slipping to the irritating man following her around the casino. She doesn't know if she'd notice being followed out here. Hopefully, even with all the lights, someone would tell her if they noticed.

Still, it was bright—like the sun was out—and all of the lights on the deck were blinding. It was more than bright enough to see everyone and everything. There were a few other people out on the upper deck, a few couples in deck chairs all bundled up—probably also hoping to see the northern lights—and a couple of older kids wandering around.

Penelope wanders around, too. There's just really nothing to see out in the dark. She can just make out the moon and some of the stars, but it's much, much too bright to see much else.

This trip had been nice, and the added benefit was that nothing really needed doing. They could languish or go on excursions, or they could wander the towns peacefully. It really took the decision-making out of the process, streamlining the hardships of travel.

And it isn't that Penelope hates it; she just wants more choice.

Maybe if they go on vacation together again, she can convince the others to go on a road trip. They can see a few states, see a few sights, and see substantially fewer guys. On a cruise, they don't have to figure out food or transportation, but she'd like to see someone, anyone, other than Neil and the other guys.

But just as Penelope knows that this is a once-in-a-lifetime trip, she also knows that others would never agree to a road trip.

Well, maybe, but Penelope will only convince them if they stay somewhere nice in between. Like, really nice, and then convince them to rough it.

Yeah, that'll go over well.

Penelope pauses on her way out of the elevator. Across from the elevators, someone had put maps. Examining it, she wonders what was hidden in the unmarked parts of the ship. Large swathes of the map don't have anything on them, at least nothing labeled. Probably because it's less safe, or crew housing or something like that, but it's still interesting to try to think about what those things are. What secrets might be hidden within the ship's belly?

That section must be the kitchens, given its distance to the dining hall. That area has to be the engines. Fortunately, the Bridge and infirmary are labeled—Penelope wonders how often people need a doctor on these kinds of trips.

Probably more than she thinks.

Hopefully, she never needs to find out.

During the walk back to her room, Penelope wonders about the locations where passengers aren't allowed and whether it would be possible to go on the Bridge or see the ship's engine room.

And wonders if she'd bump into Neil doing it.

Step after step, Penelope walks the long, plain—at points repetitive— halls of the ship, wondering first if she can take off her uncomfortable heels and then if the floor is clean enough to actually do it.

The ship is massive, and Penelope doesn't know how the crew avoids getting lost, even with all the maps. The long walk down the long, shining halls gave her plenty of time to think about how she got here.

It was nice of everyone's parents to gift them the cruise vacation as a graduation present. Teagan's parents probably came up with it; they were well-off, regularly went on cruises, and were sociable enough to plan something like this. Penelope didn't know how they got her mom on board, but it was a pleasant surprise. Her mom doesn't splurge usually, but maybe this was a ploy to find Penelope a partner.

God, she hopes her mom doesn't approve of Neil, the irritating, hobbit-ish man he is.

Talk about nightmare material.

With that thought, she's done for the evening. Done thinking, done being around other people. Just done. No more braining, thank you very much.

4

Chapter 4

"Attention all passengers and crew-"

Penelope jerks awake at the overhead announcement.

The intercom squawk comes from nowhere and everywhere, and she bolts upright, first trying to figure out where the noise is coming from and then what's being said. It takes a moment for the words to start making sense.

"-Please remain calm as we work through this together."

She blinks, patting her hair down while trying to make sense of the message. Passengers? What?

Luckily for her, it repeats twice more.

"Attention all passengers, this is your captain speaking. We have an important announcement regarding your safety and well-being. Due to unforeseen circumstances, we ask all passengers to remain in their rooms until further notice. Your cooperation is essential for the safety of everyone on board.

"We understand this may cause some inconvenience, but please know it is for your own safety. Our crew will deliver meals directly to your rooms to ensure you are well taken care of during this time. If you require any specific accommodations, please do not hesitate to contact the front desk by dialing the number provided in your room.

"Once again, all passengers are to stay in their rooms until further notice, and your meals will be delivered to you. If you require any specific accommodations, please call the front desk. Thank you for your attention, and please remain calm as we work through this situation together. Your safety is our top priority."

Silence fills the air.

Despite the shock, Penelope's eyelids are heavy. She blinks quickly, trying to wake up more and make sense of it all.

Was this like COVID again?

What happened on cruise ships when that first started? Was everyone locked in their rooms then, too?

Penelope moves slowly, hesitantly, as she looks around, trying to make sense of the sight across from her. Was this a dream? Could this be a dream?

She waits for something, anything. A sign that this is a dream or that this was a test. But nothing, not another word, follows.

It seems all they're getting is the announcement to stay in their rooms.

Melissa's bed is empty and still made, albeit not as neatly. Boring white sheets and blankets are still crisply folded but crinkled from where Courtney had sat on them. Melissa must not have come back. Or if she did, she didn't sleep in her bed. Where else would she sleep?

Maybe she was stuck with Brody?

She's fighting with the sheets, trying to pull her legs out from where they'd somehow gotten so tangled, when Courtney and Teagan rush out of the other bedroom. They're calling to her, to Melissa, Melissa, who isn't there.

Why isn't she there?

Courtney and Teagan are both sallow-skinned and look like death warmed over. When Penelope asks after Melissa, they wave her off. They're hoping a hangover cure will be delivered with the food.

"What do you think's going on? Do you think Melissa is okay?" Penelope asks, her heart fluttering in her chest. They said not to leave their rooms, but they'd need to leave their room for this, right?

One of their cabinmates is missing.

"I think that Melissa-" Teagan answers, a dry heave cutting her off, "-Melissa is with Brody. She was hanging off of him enough last night; I'd be surprised if she was anywhere else."

Courtney drapes herself on Melissa's bed, looking both very sick and like she's posing for Vogue.

"I'm gonna check in the hall," Penelope tells the other two, noticing Teagan is also in graceful repose, like a Renaissance painting. "If everyone's supposed to stay in their rooms, maybe she's coming back here."

"Doubtful..." Courtney mutters but doesn't try to stop Penelope.

Penelope pauses after unlocking the door chain. Slowly, she pulls it open, unable to control how her eyebrows raise when the door opens without resistance. Somehow, somewhy, Penelope half expects it to be super locked or something. It creaks loudly, but no alarms go off, so it isn't trapped—at least, not obviously.

Poking her head out, Penelope looks around. The halls are empty for once. Nothing too unusual; just, there isn't anyone around. For once. Penelope considers calling for Melissa (in case she got lost, before deciding against it.

She wonders if they're actually doing what they're supposed to. Maybe they have learned as a society.

Then again, if other people are wandering around where she couldn't see them, she wouldn't know.

Penelope sticks her head out further, looking for any sign of movement—any sign of life—but she doesn't see anything or anyone.

She wonders about Melissa. If she isn't in there, what will happen to her? Will she be brought to them? Will she get in trouble? When will all

22

of that happen?

What time was it now?

A yawn splits her face as though the acknowledgment of the time likely being too damn early enough to put her to sleep again. Anyway, Penelope thought, it was a problem for a later, more alert version of her.

Melissa's probably safe; she's gotta be. And once Penelope is more awake, she'll come up with a plan. Maybe she can call the front desk and see if they can tell her anything.

But for now, she wants to go back to bed.

Everyone's probably calling now anyway. Better to rest more than clog the lines.

5

Chapter 5

Penelope's about ready to try putting her head through a wall to see if that would help with the noise or the situation.

It couldn't do much harm at any rate.

"But he always calls! And he always calls right now. He has every day that we've been on this stupid ship; why would he stop today?" Teagan's freaking out over the lack of internet—which they'd lost some time last night—wasn't helping the pounding in Penelope's head.

The others had gone back to sleep, and once she woke again, Penelope had a little time to herself. She spent it on hold, waiting to speak to someone about why they were on lockdown, and the hold time didn't seem to go down at all.

Even a little bit.

Actually, it might have gone up a couple of times. It hadn't seemed long when they'd first put Penelope on hold, but now it seemed like hours.

But it's been more than an hour since she'd gotten up, and now Courtney and Teagan are up, too, and they have decided they are going to be problems.

Penelope's problems, particularly.

As much as she wants to tell them to cut it out, she hopes it'll be understandable or not dangerous but inconvenient.

"Maybe he's just busy?" Teagan says more to herself than the others. "I can't access anything! No Google, no Insta, no nothing! Why isn't the internet working?"

Penelope has to fight to keep from snapping, "Maybe there's just too many people on the ship."

"No, I mean, it's not like there's more people than usual?" Courtney hesitantly argues, voice soft but still insistent, "I mean, no one else is here that wasn't here yesterday and the day before, so it's gotta be something else. Right?"

"Unless people were working off the wifi, they got in the towns, so this is the first time everyone is actually on the ship's internet." Penelope sighs, the overly cheery music from the phone grinding its way into her headache. She was sure she knew the entire song on the hold music. "It's not the end of the world; the ship's Wi-Fi is probably just overloaded by everyone. At worst, we'll be back in port in a couple of days, and you can check up on everything you missed then."

Courtney pouts, "But how am I supposed to check in with my followers and mutuals? They're gonna miss me."

Penelope rubs her forehead, feeling muscles fighting the attempts to move them. "Do we have anything for a headache?"

Teagan shakes her head, "I brought my little kit, but we used it all when Melissa fell down those stairs in Ketchikan."

"But that was, like, day one!" Penelope struggles not to whine, but she can feel it creeping out. "You don't have anything else?"

"Nope!" Teagan answers, popping the 'P,' "How is the cell service AND the internet out?"

"The cell service is probably piggybacked off the internet on the ship," Courtney tells her, beating Penelope. "Why do you think everyone's locked away today?"

"Who knows, maybe it's a noro outbreak or something. I heard another ship had like, a third of the passengers down with it." Teagan answers.

"Yeah, but that doesn't explain why they locked everyone away." Penelope answers, cracking her neck, "There were still passengers on that ship who were out and about."

"And? Maybe our ship has more cases."

"If that were the case, they probably would have kept us in port or something. There's probably something else going on." Penelope pauses, "Maybe it's something dangerous?"

"Like what?"

"I don't know." Groaning, Penelope rubs her eyes, setting the phone down for the time being. The cheery hold music was still too loud from this distance, "I just don't think they'd lock everyone away for something like that when it would probably be easier to lock away the people who were sick."

Penelope keeps rubbing her eyes, worried but not sure what to add.

"Look, you're freaking me out-" Teagan interrupts the heavy silence, "-and I want to call my boyfriend. You're obviously not getting anywhere waiting on hold. Let me call Colby, and then you can get back on hold forever."

"I've already been on hold for like an hour, no way."

"Come on, you're going to be on hold forever anyway. Just let me call Colby, and then you can get back on hold for approximately forever!" Teagan whines, a nasal pitch to it that drives Penelope nuts.

"No way, Teagan. I've already been on hold for an hour. I don't want to wait even more."

"Everyone's probably calling right now. You might as well wait a couple hours and then call when all the people who've given up are off the lines."

"Us included, huh?"

"Well, yeah. But come on, Penelope." Teagan weedles, "You were planning to be locked on the balcony the whole time anyway."

"Yeah, I was planning that, wasn't I..." Penelope rubs her eyes. This didn't change her plans much; add Teagan and Courtney whining in the main cabin to it.

Teagan nods when Penelope looks at her, obviously fighting to avoid making grabby hands at the phone.

"You really think that we'll be able to call the front desk in a couple hours?"

"At the latest." Teagan really looks like she's about to cry, "Please, Pen, let me just call Colby?"

Penelope groans, "Fine, I guess."

Teagan rushes to the phone, dialing her boyfriend's number.

Penelope doesn't move or have the chance to do so. Teagan practically pins in her place to dial the phone.

But the phone goes to a busy signal.

The harsh klaxon startles both of them, but it doesn't stop Teagan. She calls again and gets the busy signal again.

She's not looking at Penelope and barely budges as she tries to get out. All of her focus is on the phone as she gets increasingly upset she can't contact her boyfriend.

It doesn't work, and after a few tries, she wants to try again on the other phones.

Courtney only argues for a second before letting Teagan have it, and they all listen as it goes straight to the busy signal again. Penelope hands hers over, knowing there's no point in fighting.

But hers doesn't work any better than the others.

Penelope feels like she's the only one concerned about why they're locked in or finding out more about what's keeping them in place for now. She wonders if anyone will be by with food soon and how much food they have on hand for everyone.

She read about it happening on one of the forums. Some ship in the Bahamas or something where a large portion of the vessel had caught COVID, and they'd have to keep everyone in their rooms. But that was a different situation, right?

It can't be the situation here, and if it is, wouldn't it be better to tell everyone? Instead of being creepy and quiet about it?

Maybe she was overthinking things, but why wouldn't they tell the passengers anything?

Wouldn't it be better to tell them so they don't flood the front desk with calls, just like this? Or go down there themselves because of the long hold?

She watches Courtney fight with her computer and phone and Teagan fight with the cabin phone. She wonders how long it will be before they want to go down to the front desk themselves.

What was going on here?

And why weren't they being told anything?

6

Chapter 6

A swift but polite knock on the door startles Penelope.

From her place on her bed, she can see the living area, where Courtney and Teagan rest on the couch. But neither seem to be moving enough to cause the knock or show they'd heard it. Her phone says it's nearly noon, way, way later than she'd be expecting, well, anything.

Taking a moment to unlock the door, Penelope sticks her head out.

The mystery knocker is already gone when Penelope opens the door. In front of the door are more covered trays.

Penelope looks around, stepping out a pace to see if there's any sign of the mystery knocker. She wonders if they'd run off because they were unable—or simply unwilling—to answer their questions.

A younger teen across the hall peeks his head out shortly after her, looking as confused as Penelope feels.

Being the first new person Penelope's seen in days, she probably looks him over more intently than she would normally. He's frankly cherubic, with soft blond curls framing a youthful face still round and baby fat. He's dressed for lazing around in sweatpants and a way too big T-shirt that dwarfs the small frame under it.

Before either can ask a question, a banshee-like screech comes from within his cabin. "Charlie! You close that door right now! What are you thinking? I told you to stay away from it!"

"They left us food, Mrs. S! Keep your pants on!" The boy picks up the trays, "Or put them back on, jeez."

Penelope can't help the snort that escapes her. She smiles at the boy, who smiles back, rolling his eyes a bit before retreating.

Still smiling, Penelope grabs their trays—which feel lighter today than they did the day before—and balances them as she closes the door.

"Oh my god, is that food?" Courtney asks as all three descend on their food like starving wolves, which isn't far from the truth.

The eggs were cold and bland, lacking salt or pepper. The bread wasn't even toasted. And it couldn't taste better.

The others probably ate a bit more recently, probably something from the bar. Not that it really mattered. They had a mild concern, so they probably held off on their complaints for a little longer.

Probably a mean thought, but she was really hangry.

They split the fourth platter, knowing it was for Melissa, but it wasn't like they could save it for her; she wasn't here now.

Penelope cleans up—thankful for something to do—dropping the trays off and looking around again. They seem to be the first to finish; at least, they're the only ones who've placed their trays back outside. The feeling of aloneness strikes Penelope. She wonders where everyone else is, why they aren't out there making noise, something.

Up to this point, she couldn't go anywhere on this godforsaken ship without bumping into people. Now...

Silence, stillness, solitude.

Back into the room. She isn't going to get them in trouble by wandering around, and there's bound to be another announcement sooner or later. And then they'll have more to work with. It would all be okay. Or they'd be home soon.

Courtney goes out to sun herself while the sun's on their side, and

Teagan goes to take a nap.

When they wake up, both complain about their lack of internet and then move to how they have nothing to do, locked in their rooms. Penelope ignores them. They're bored, and they'd planned to be out and about or play on their phones for most of the trip.

With food in her system, Penelope feels she has a second wind. She can and will be able to spend the unbelievably long hours she needs on the phone. Or, with luck, everyone else wouldn't spend more time on the phone. But when Penelope calls, there's no answer, just more hold music.

Penelope nearly hangs up again, grabbing her book. She had all the time in the world, and she'd been planning to do this anyway. So, she might as well camp out in the last bit of sun they'd probably be getting instead of hiding, waiting on the phone.

The ding of the overhead announcement came, once again, at the right time to startle the crap out of her. "Ladies and gentlemen, this is your captain speaking. Firstly, I want to extend my gratitude to all of you for your cooperation in remaining in your cabins during this time. Your patience and understanding are greatly appreciated."

The captain drones on, but there's something in his voice that raises the hair on the back of Penelope's neck. An almost quiver that's been suppressed.

"We are still on schedule and will be making landfall in Vancouver at the expected time. However, I kindly remind you that it is currently prohibited to leave your cabins. We ask for your continued cooperation in this matter."

It's still there, but whatever emotion's trying to escape has been firmly stomped on.

"Once we reach our destination, disembarkation will be based on your groups. Please wait for your group to be called before leaving your cabin to ensure a smooth and orderly disembarking process for everyone.

"We thank you for your attention and cooperation. And we appreciate your understanding and look forward to a safe and efficient disembarkation process."

They wouldn't be able to get through, not for a long while.

Even though she knows she shouldn't, Penelope gives up. Hangs up. There's probably a lot of people—more than before—calling the front desk now.

She couldn't believe they were stuck in their cabins until they returned to port.

Penelope returned to her book—it was pretty much all that was left—and wondered if they'd be allowed out in their groups again.

Even though they had lots to complain about, the others' main focus was still the lack of internet.

When they were planning the trip, Courtney pushed for the internet package even though it was way more expensive rather than going without for a few days.

She'd wanted to post everything as it was happening and keep up with her boo.

They'd all politely ignored that Courtney had broken up with her the week before the trip. But Courtney had taken even more 'fire' pictures than usual to show off how happy she was and how hot she looked. How glad she was to be on this trip with her friends and to meet all these people. Especially when meeting all the people, she'd probably take more photos with strangers than before.

That was an emotional mess that Penelope wouldn't touch with a ten-foot pole.

Penelope reads her books, all of them things she'd picked up along the way, most of them Alaska-themed. For now, she's avoiding thinking too hard about any issues she finds in any of the books, trying to just let the story fill the time. She's finishing them faster than she'd like, the first one over with sooner than she expected, and then moved on to one that was deceptively wordy for its size.

It's a little easier to breathe outside.

It's just her, the wind, and the sound of the waves far, far below.

And then it's Teagan, too.

After some pointed complaints, heavy sighs, and gentle nudges, she lets Teagan read one of her books. Even though she complains the whole time.

"I can't believe you're reading this," Teagan says, a third of the way into one Penelope had barely looked at but to buy, focusing more that it had been written by a local author than anything else.

"What?"

"This, it's filth, practically from the first chapter." Teagan's still reading it, though.

"If it's that bad, stop."

Teagan hunches in her seat more, holding the book so close to her face that Penelope is surprised she can read it. "I didn't say it was bad; I said it was filth."

Penelope shakes her head, trying to focus on her book, "Then why are you complaining?"

"It's still filthy." Teagan doesn't seem bothered, though, sticking her nose further into the book if possible.

Courtney chooses then to wander outside, though there are no more chairs.

"There's still no service." Courtney groans, leaning over the balcony railing like a brooding protagonist.

"We know, Courtney," Penelope says, trying to avoid looking so she doesn't get drawn into the conversation further.

Courtney groans again, back dipping, stretching like a ballerina, "I'm so booooooored."

Teagan groans, "We know, Courtney."

"Want to try calling the front desk again?" Penelope offers, flipping the page.

"No, I bet everyone's calling there still." Courtney sits with her back against the railing.

It's a little easier for Penelope to breathe with Courtney here, too. Some of the tightness in her chest falls away, and she can relax more with her friends somewhere she can see them.

Well, two of her friends where she can see them.

But she still worries about Melissa. Worries about her friend, who's too far away from her and the rest of them.

Even though she hasn't been here since they got locked in, Penelope wishes she'd spent more time listening to Melissa. They can't call to check on her without the other room number, and they don't even know if they could call with the lines busy.

Penelope hopes she's safe, wherever she is, that she's somewhere with a little room to walk around, like in their cabin.

Courtney also digs through the bag of books, eventually pulling out one about the history of float plane pilots. That one was supposed to be a gift, but she could have it if it was Courtney's first choice.

More of the day passes. The sun stays up so long here it seems impossible to guess the time. The shadows it casts go on and on without really changing. It's beautiful and warmer in the direct sun than in the room. It's one of the reasons she stays out as long as she does, eyeing the clouds that rest on the horizon.

Hunger gnawing at her stomach, Penelope checks the door around their normal dinner time, thankful for her alarm.

She finds the trays have been dropped off. But they're cold, probably dropped off much earlier in the day, making it all the harder to eat even when they are as hungry as they are. The spread is minimal, barely enough to count as a meal.

Courtney wants to complain, but Penelope convinces her it's not worth it. They hadn't heard the knock, and there had to be problems delivering this much food all over the ship every day.

After eating, Penelope's full of anxious energy and not much else.

She tries not to pace. Other people would probably be irritated by it, and even if she couldn't hear the people upstairs, she didn't want to annoy the people below.

It doesn't stop Teagan, who paces while she tries all their phones again to call Colby.

He never picks up, and it goes to the busy signal each time.

Eventually, Teagan goes to bed. With nothing left to do, sleep is the last reasonable option, even if the sun is still up.

Courtney follows. She takes Melissa's bed, claiming she wants to be able to hear the door so their next meal is nice and hot.

Penelope doesn't sleep. She can't. Even if she wanted to, her mind spins a million miles an hour.

Nighttime comes, eventually.

She leaves the lights off and searches the darkness, looking for any sign of other people. Ships they might be passing, maybe floating platforms. Something to show that it's not just here in out here. But there are no visible lights off the ship, just a dim glow in the distance.

In the dark, she feels all alone.

There don't seem to be many people out on their balconies. She can spot a few, though. But none of them try to talk to her.

Maybe it's the timezone; she knows it's late. Later than Penelope would ever stay up at home and probably much later than most of these people usually would.

It's cold, getting colder, but Penelope doesn't move. She's half sure she can see her breath.

On cold nights like this, they might see the northern lights.

At least, that's what her mom had told her.

When her mom told her about this surprise trip, Penelope was really shocked. She'd never expected anything like this.

Her mom had been so excited for her that she stayed on the phone with her while she packed, telling her everything she'd learned about the Tongass Rainforest and everything they might see on their trip.

Her mom was right; it was way better in person.

Seeing the glow of the northern lights across the sky, even with the lights on all across the ship, was much better than anything she'd imagined.

She hopes she'll get to tell her soon.

7

Chapter 7

There are more announcements a couple hours after the sun comes up.

It's more of the same: once again, reminding people to stay in their rooms, thanking them for their patience, and reminding them to call the front desk with any questions or concerns.

Penelope tries to reassure herself that everything will be fine, but even though she's trying, the worries remain. Nothing said it would all be explained eventually.

Nothing that promised they'd be able to come out of their rooms eventually. Just more of the same. It was driving her a bit mad, more than a bit mad. Or maybe it was the sleep deprivation that was succeeding in driving her mad.

Penelope ends her unofficial vigil when Teagan gets out of bed, looks still looking as tired as Penelope feels. Either unable to sleep or woken by her worries.

Even though thoughts still spin like Beyblades in her mind, Penelope falls asleep almost as soon as her head hits the pillow.

...— — —... ...— — —... ...— — —...

A few fitful hours later, Penelope feels, if possible, less rested than she did when she laid down.

The others are worried, too; both also hadn't slept well. They avoid that too, though. Why they hadn't been sleeping as hard to understand as what was going on or what they would do next.

Food only comes once that day, closer to mid-afternoon. Again, there were four platters that they silently split.

Courtney still took plenty of pictures, first of the food and then some of their snack store before letting Teagan and Penelope eat it. Even though it was obvious that Courtney was doing this as a cover, to keep herself calm or at least feign normality.

Aside from the approved menus, everything on the ship costs an arm and a leg. Penelope picked up about as much food as she could carry while in Kodiak, sure that she and the others would want to graze more than their wallets would care for.

Now Penelope is just thankful that she'd bought easy to eat and fast foods. Teagan and Courtney were happy to pool their food with her, which made it all go a little farther.

Overall, it's a decent pile.

It's not perfect, but it's at least food—maybe enough to last a couple of days in addition to the singular daily meals from the kitchens.

Courtney chatters with the other two about what she should label the pictures when they get internet again. She's sure it's only a matter of time it's up and running again, so it's only a matter of time until she can get everything all set up and posted.

Letting herself be distracted by the conversation, Penelope ignores Courtney's tight voice and darting eyes.

Penelope was making serious headway through her pile of books; even if she had plenty of others, she wanted to make sure she'd have some light reading for the flights home.

Now the others are getting worried, really worried. There haven't been any announcements since the one that morning.

Teagan tries all their phones again, trying to reach Colby. Really, it made sense none of them had a signal. Penelope wonders how bad the international charges were going to be on her next bill, knowing no matter how much it ended up being, it would probably be worth it for her friend having something to do now.

Penelope checks the door around dinner time again. Even though Courtney's been camping out next to it.

But there's no food. Their dishes haven't even been taken away.

She tries not to freak out about the lack of food, information, or space.

One meal a day is probably still enough for everyone. It's not comfortable, but it's technically enough.

Penelope wonders why the trays haven't been picked up yet.

Maybe it was the flu or something like it. Or maybe they'd miscalculated how much food they'd need and they didn't want to worry people or risk looting or the passengers trying to find their own food.

That seems less likely, though.

At the end of summer, they've made this journey so many times they have to know how much is enough for everyone. And if they didn't, they probably have stores for situations like this.

It didn't matter much anyway.

In less than a week, they'd be out of here and they'd never have to think about this again, except when reminiscing.

8

Chapter 8

On the third day, rain poured down outside in thick, heavy sheets that looked unreal.

Penelope's stomach scrapped at her insides, leaving her raw and sharp, and she could tell that it was getting to the others, too. They all tried not to be snippy at each other. Being trapped in their cabin for so long without entertainment wasn't helping either.

Penelope tried to remain civil before locking herself on the deck. Armored with the thick, heavy winter coat her mom had gifted her to tell her about this trip—an underutilized gift with the warm weather and clear skies—and the blankets off Melissa's bed.

Rain be damned.

It was a wet kind of cold that seeped through the layers, curling around Penelope's toes and fingers until she tucked her hands and feet away. At least the balcony was covered, and there wasn't a lot of wind, though it still persistently raked over her face and ears like it was trying to find a crack in her warm armor.

The rain, thankfully, stayed outside the small balcony for the most part.

The heavy, pounding rain and whipping, cold wind was more than enough to keep the others in the cabin and away from Penelope.

In retrospect, connecting the bedrooms to a shared living space wasn't the best idea. On the off chance they ever went on a cruise again, Penelope would have to cough up the extra money to make sure she didn't have to share a space with them. If they ever went on a cruise together, that was.

The only good thing was that Melissa wasn't here; she'd probably be complaining most of the lot of them, but for now, she was her boy-toy's problem. Penelope still hoped she was safe wherever she was.

Only when the sun goes down—changing the weather along with it—dousing Penelope in driving rain and deep, bone-aching cold, does she give up and go inside. Between the cold, the wet, and the gnawing in her gut turning into sharp pains, she has to admit defeat.

She's sure that there's got to be something to eat, probably something cold, rubbery, and disgusting, but better than nothing.

Courtney perks up from Melissa's bed, "Here's our shivering beauty."

"Where's the food?" Penelope asks, looking around the room for the trays or anything they might have eaten while she's been in her self-imposed exile.

"That's what I'm wondering, too." Courtney tells her, "There hadn't been any food delivered today. Like at all."

Penelope finds it hard to believe. They haven't been brought anything on the third day of confinement? "Nothing?"

"Nothing," Courtney confirms.

Now is the time to worry.

Penelope sticks her head out in the hall again, but there's nothing and no one out there. The trays with their dishes from the day before were still there, too, and it looked like that was true for the whole hallway.

"Have you two eaten anything?" Penelope asks, wondering if there is even anything left for her.

Courtney pulls out the reusable bag where they'd stashed all the food, which looked lighter than when they'd been combining food the day before, "Some. Teagan wanted to be careful with how much we ate. Something about how starving is worse if it's sudden."

Penelope's drooling over the bag, but she doesn't pull out as much as she wants, as much as her stomach demands. She knows her eyes are probably bigger than her stomach even now. Penelope pulls out a couple bags of chips and a little vacuum-sealed pack of smoked salmon. It's supposed to be for her mom, but she'll understand.

Courtney seems to take Penelope's attempts to not inhale her food as her cue to leave, returning to Melissa's bed and curling up.

Penelope tries not to watch her. She knows there's been something between the two, good and bad. She knows that Courtney wishes she could take back everything that's happened. But there isn't much to do about it, not while they're stuck here and Melissa's stuck elsewhere.

Teagan comes out a little later, hair mussed, damp, and exhausted, and sits beside Penelope. She doesn't say anything—neither of them do—she just sits, staring at the phone in the room.

Later, minutes or hours, Courtney joins them again, but no one exchanges a word. They look between each other and the phone, their gazes always drawn back to it as though pulled by an invisible force.

It had to have been long enough. So, even though it's near midnight, they try to call the front desk.

They've never gotten through before, but that doesn't stop them; it doesn't even slow them down.

This time, there's just a busy signal. No hold music.

They try again.

Again, they get the busy signal.

Each time they try, they get the busy signal.

They keep trying anyway.

They try and keep trying for hours, hoping beyond hope that they'll get through.

All through the dark storm of the night, after the dismal gray of the cloud lightened again. There's no answer and no announcement.

Penelope doesn't try to hide her fear, and neither do the other girls. They keep taking turns, giving up the phone long enough for someone else to make the call, then snatching it back as soon as possible, hoping, praying, they'd get an answer soon.

Soon, soon, soon.

9

Chapter 9

Penelope watches through the balcony windows as the rain continues dumping buckets outside.

As far as she can tell, they're moving in the same direction they have been, at least throughout the night and most of the previous day. It could be the right direction; she would think this was right, but how was she supposed to know?

The captain had said they were going the right way, but that didn't mean much if they couldn't confirm it.

Penelope didn't sleep much; every time she fell asleep, she was startled awake. She was sure she could hear screams every so often. But she couldn't hear any screaming when she checked the hall or when she focused intently on listening while in bed. The wind covered nearly all sounds if she opened the door to check outside.

Unable to tell where the screams were coming from, Penelope chose to stay awake. Was it in her head? What was making her hear such ghastly noises? Why would she be imagining them?

Worse, what if it was happening and no one was doing anything?

The screams weren't always the same volume, and they weren't the same noise each time. Each was seemingly different, maybe from different people.

Was that better or worse?

Teagan and Courtney join Penelope in the tiny living space once more, and Teagan goes straight to their food pile.

"We need to do something." Penelope breaks the silence, unable to stand watching Teagan sort through their meager remaining food, repeatedly checking the nutrition labels and sorting them into piles.

"We're almost out of food," Teagan offers.

"We're almost out of food, and we'll be here another three days at least," Courtney adds.

"What do we have left?"

"Not even close to enough for the next few days. Some cans of salmon we can't get into-" She knocks the can on the floor hard enough that Penelope's worried it'll bust. "-some kelp salsa that I don't know if it's actually food or not, and then a couple candy bars that I'm pretty sure are novelty candy bars that aren't actually meant for eating."

Thinking momentarily, Penelope asks, "Any way we can get into the canned salmon?"

"Maybe if we had a can opener," Teagan says, "but they confiscated mine on the way in."

"Ugh," Penelope says, the others echoing her.

Teagan keeps packing and unpacking the snacks, like that'll make more of them appear. She sorts over and over again by proteins, carbs, and calories.

"Do you think we'll be okay?" Courtney asks after a few minutes of silence.

"It's going to be a few days until we get to port." Teagan says, "Maybe they just missed our wing or something? And they'll bring more to make up for it?"

"Come on," Penelope snaps, "There's gotta be some kind of system they follow, and don't you think they would have made some kind of announcement if that was the case?"

Teagan's near tears, "Why haven't I been able to get in contact with Colby?

"Teagan, we've been over this-"

"I mean, we haven't really! It might be the lack of signal, but we've had intermittent signal for most of the time we've been in the inner passage." Teagan starts pacing, "I think we're being cut off somehow."

"Or, more likely, we're just out of range for all the internet and cell service providers," Penelope tells them, all energy, all fight leaving her.

"But the ship isn't set up to intentionally cut people off, so it has to be something else. Right?" Teagan stops to look at them. "But they have to be cutting us off somehow 'cause we're supposed to have internet and stuff the whole time."

"But what would be doing that? Why?" Penelope asks.

Courtney sounds sure when she speaks, even if her brows are furrowed. She usually wouldn't do that; she's always trying to avoid making any lines on her face. "If we had internet, we could see what was going on. You know, read the news, talk to people outside this stupid cruise ship that's keeping us away from the rest of the world."

"And?" Penelope asks, interested in the idea of a conspiracy if nothing else, but it's better than going talking about the food situation again. "You think there's something going on?"

"I mean, probably. There has to be something they don't want us to know about."

"You know," Teagan offers, "I think it might have something to do with the riots down south and in New York."

"Oh, yeah..." Now, Penelope remembers that some bill just passed, and people everywhere were unhappy with it. She didn't listen to the news, but she'd seen snippets about it everywhere online. Everyone focused on how many people were rioting over it, "It's been over a week, though. I'm pretty sure that would have been resolved by now, wouldn't it?

"It doesn't matter if it's resolved, Penelope!" Teagan hisses, "What matters is we don't know; we don't know anything! We can't even leave the cabin!"

"Fine! Let's just go down to the front desk. I doubt we're the only ones who are hungry and worried about everything." Penelope stands abruptly. "Come on, at least we'll get out of this stupid cabin."

"There's an order to stay in place, though," Courtney says, wringing her hands as her gaze darts between Penelope and the door.

Penelope is tired of this and honestly a little tired of her friends, "There's no food, and there hasn't been in days. We don't know what's going on. We need answers, and we need help."

"Are we really going to go down there?" Courtney asks.

"Yes!" Teagan says, grabbing her coat. "We need to find out what's going on!"

10

Chapter 10

"This can't be a good idea," Courtney's voice quivers as she watches Penelope get dressed in a longer skirt she'd brought on this trip. She didn't know what was happening, but she hadn't shaved in days and wasn't about to do it just to talk to the people at the front desk.

"It's the only one we've got right now, Courtney. If we don't leave, we're going to starve." Penelope tells her, wishing she could be softer. "To death."

"But at least we're safe here. And even with whatever's going on, we'll be home soon." Courtney's looking between Penelope and the door. "It's only a few more days, right?"

"It's a couple days we may not have," Penelope tells her.

"Courtney, do you know what happens when you starve to death?" Teagan interrupts, apparently not feeling the need to be soft.

It takes Courtney a moment to mutter a soft denial.

"It's one of the worst ways you can die. It's slow, painful, and so long, so, so long." Teagan starts before getting into the details of what happens when you starve. Even if they made it through the next few days, they'd get sicker and weaker. Too weak to do anything eventually, at risk of eating themselves to death later because they won't be able to

48

stop themselves.

Surprisingly, Courtney's all for it after that lecture and terrible, terrible-sounding fate, rushing to get dressed even as sick as she is.

Now that they're in agreement, they come up with a fairly simple plan: They'll all go down to the desk, see if they can find out where Brody and Neil are staying—contact Melissa—and find out what's going on, why there haven't been food deliveries, and hopefully, get some food, and then go back to their room.

It's a perfect, simple plan.

Teagan leads them, initially walking normally. But the further they go without passing anyone, the more freaked out everyone gets.

The walk toward the ship's center is long, incredibly long. After all their time in their cabin, it's easy to forget how big the ship is. Penelope's heard it called a floating hotel before, but that wasn't right; it was more like a floating city.

Long hallways lead to the center of the ship. Colorless, lifeless, utterly devoid of humanity. It's so very different from before. From any of the other times, they'd walked around the ship. Around them is the echo of people somewhere, but there's no one nearby. Are the footsteps their own, or are they the sounds of other people? Are they down different halls, just out of sight? Or are they really alone?

Every other time, people—children, adults, old ladies, everyone and anyone—have been laughing, talking, existing, and making so much noise.

This time, though, it's completely silent but for the sounds of footsteps.

They talk initially, theorizing, thinking, just keeping their minds off the strangeness—anything to keep the awful silence away. It's easy enough to say that they're almost certain, almost sure, that the only reason there's no one else is that they're all supposed to be staying in their cabins, but that only works for a while, only works until they all get too nervous again.

But what stops them isn't the silence, lack of people, or the incredibly long, blank hallways.

It's the blood spatters.

The bodies.

The thick, coppery scent of blood, the sickly smell of decay already wafting from the bodies.

Halfway down the ship, so close to their room and still so far away, would they have heard them?

Were these people the source of the screams?

Dozens of bodies lay in the hall, halfway through doors, their blood splattering the walls. Some of them—Penelope hopes it's only some of them—are unrecognizable as human, with only the shreds of clothing, watches, and jewelry still attached, bloody messes identifying them as once human.

Penelope is the first to speak: "We have to go back. We have to go back right now!"

Their room is almost at the back of the ship and hard to reach. But there's still other rooms around them, other people. People who might know what to do.

At least in theory.

Whatever was going on was so much worse than she'd thought, so, so much worse.

She and the others should have known better. They should have just stayed in their cabin; it was safe there.

There are so many bodies.

So many of them, too many of them.

People who've left their rooms. And look at what they walked into.

It wasn't safe; they had to get out of here.

Courtney's already moving away, clutching at Teagan's arm, "Yeah, we gotta go back right now; we have to. I can't believe-"

She cuts herself off with a gag.

Penelope hadn't realized she'd said it out loud, but it didn't matter.

Passing their dry-heaving friend to her, Teagan checks a couple of the rooms, stepping over most of the viscera while looking for signs of life or what might have caused this. But she doesn't go too far in. They don't know what did this, or if it's still nearby.

... — — — ... ... — — — ... ... — — — ...

Penelope doesn't remember getting back to the room. One second, they're surrounded by viscera, and the next, she's rubbing Courtney's back while she heaves over the toilet in their cabin.

"It's horrible," Courtney says in the breaths of air she gets between heaves. "I can't believe-"

Penelope's mind is working overdrive. Disgust and nausea, overridden by shock, "What could have done this? What the hell did this?"

"That looks like something from one of my textbooks; this can't be real life. It can't be real life." Teagan is pacing around the room, "No, it- it had to be a mistake! Maybe they're running some kind of drill?"

"A drill, Teagan? Really?" Penelope snaps, "This isn't a stupid drill! This is- this is real life. That- that- Mhm. There's something terrible going on. I don't know what it is. They wouldn't make this up. They couldn't- not without some kind of warning, right?"

Courtney is too busy dry-heaving to respond.

Teagan pauses in the doorway, "There's something so much worse going on. But what are we going to do?"

Question of the night, what are they going to do?

They'll probably starve to the point of being too weak to get off the ship if they wait. And they don't know if they'll be able to get off the ship any other way.

They have to get somewhere safe, maybe the bridge? The infirmary?

But what if they ran into whatever attacked all those people? To whatever killed them?

None of them know how to fight.

It wasn't something Penelope had ever thought she'd need. The area she lived in was safe, and her college campus was well-patrolled. It wasn't like she was a big risk-taker. She didn't even go out drinking.

And now something on here was shredding people.

"Well? What do we do?" Teagan half pleads.

"I don't know, we'll come up with something." Penelope starts pacing herself.

She feels sick, worse than sick; like if she stops moving, the whole damn ship is going to fall out from underneath her. If she focuses on the sharp fluttering sensation in her chest, she's going to cry or scream or shatter into a million pieces.

They need to leave, but they still need to find out what happened. They don't know what they'll find if they go, and if there's that much blood and bodies, there's no telling what could be doing it. They don't know what's on the ship with them, but it's dangerous.

"We have to get out of here. Somehow, maybe—maybe not the front desk. Maybe the bridge? There has to be somewhere we can go," Penelope says, trying to remember what to do if there were instructions in case of emergencies like this.

"Why? It's too dangerous-" Courtney groans from where she's still worshiping the porcelain throne or whatever cruise ship toilets were made of.

"We need weapons. At least that much, something." Penelope thinks, Weapons, weapons, what could we use?

"But they took everything away. Even the pocket knife Teagan brought." Courtney complains.

So what could they use?

"Let's see," Penelope looks around the room, taking it all in. There's a little desk. Maybe they could break it apart. Or the table? It didn't look like it was bolted to the wall too firmly; at the very least, they might be able to get some of the legs off, if not all. "We just have to break some things. Just a chair, maybe the table."

"You want us to destroy the furniture?" Courtney half gasps.

"You want to die instead?"

"I think I'm going to be sick," Courtney says.

Penelope shakes her head and grabs one of the chairs from their small table. She gets a good grip on the back and then adjusts slightly. She's sure she can do this; she just has to.

Would it be as easy as it was in the movies? Or would breaking the chair be its own battle?

Well, she was about to find out.

Slamming the chair into the ground wasn't easy, easier than she thought, but not easy. And it didn't just fall apart like they do in the movies. Penelope could feel the vibration of the impact all the way through her arms and into her back, shaking her to her core, but she couldn't stop now. She slams it into the ground again. This time, hearing the fracture and feeling it give a little more.

One more time, just one more, it should be enough.

Slamming it down again, it finally shatters almost perfectly—almost like they do in the movies. She rips off one of the legs, hands it to Teagan, and then rips off another.

Courtney stands; Penelope hands her the chair leg and rips off another.

"We don't have another choice. We just have to do what we can." Penelope tells her. "And I'd like to see them get mad at us for this."

Courtney weakly chuckles. She still looks like she's going to throw up, but they hadn't had anything to eat in, well, too long now. There's nothing to come up.

Now, at least they're halfway armed. They have a fighting chance.

They head down again, carefully, much, much more carefully than before.

Now looking for anything even slightly out of place, anything that might tell them what was going on or warn them before they get attacked.

11

Chapter 11

They stand at the edge of the blood splatters once more, all of them avoiding looking at the bodies. Penelope doesn't know who started it, but they're arguing about where they need to go, the sickly sweet metallic smell so strong it covers up all other scents. It's so thick in the air that it weighs on Penelope's tongue.

"Come on, we're not that far from the front desk," Teagan tells them, avoiding looking at where the blood has spattered.

"No, we need food. There's not going to be anyone there anyway." Penelope argues, her voice lowered to avoid the attention of whatever had done all this, on the off chance it was still nearby.

"Maybe there's somewhere we can go to signal for help?" Courtney says, still green but not gagging anymore. She looks like she'd like to lean against one of the walls, but the gore reaches too high for her to do that.

"The front desk might have some kind of explanation, though," Teagan reasons. "Maybe some posted signage?"

"An explanation doesn't mean much to me right now. We need to eat." Penelope tries to make her tone allow no argument, but that doesn't stop Teagan.

"Maybe we can find food at the front desk?" Teagan tries, but it's obvious she knows it's a weak argument.

"We're more likely to find information in the kitchens," Penelope tells her.

"Actually," Courtney says, "I'm going to agree with Penelope. I'm starving."

Teagan throws her hands up, giving in, and gestures for Penelope to lead.

Trying to remember the map she'd looked at a few days ago, Penelope heads to where she hopes the kitchens are.

Their stomachs push them on.

There's still a faint smell of something in the air, maybe something sweet? It's definitely something that smells like food, something a million times better than the thick, syrupy scent of blood.

She's so hungry.

There are a couple of half-hidden doors to the hidden parts of the ship that only the crew were supposed to be in. The doors aren't truly hidden, but they're not marked the same as areas the passengers were allowed in, and they're the same color as the walls, making them harder to spot. The doors are hidden off the main sections; Penelope is aware that the crew quarters are mostly under sea level and assumed that most of the other rooms the crew spent a lot of time in when they weren't working were probably underwater, too.

They slip into one of the halls, finding them dark except for minimal emergency lighting.

Penelope and the others use their phones as flashlights in the dark, which barely light up the halls. Fortunately, they find a map almost immediately, letting them orient themselves and find the kitchens.

Which are higher up in the ship than Penelope thought.

It makes sense that it would be right off the dining room; she shouldn't be blamed for that, despite Teagan's fiery stare burning into the side of her head as she tries to memorize the map.

Courtney takes a picture and Penelope coughs. She maybe forgot that was an option.

But it was still higher up in the ship than she thought.

Adding even more time till they could get something to eat. Till they could get out of here.

Of course, because they were traumatized enough, strewn throughout the back halls are far, far too many bodies.

They sneak through the halls.

It doesn't prevent them from seeing more bodies, all horrifically damaged, along the way. But it might keep them safe from whatever's left bodies strewn all over the place.

Penelope leads, one hand holding her shirt over her mouth, the other clutching her skirt and phone while attempting to avoid the worst of the viscera. She really should have changed earlier. Fitting her feet into the gaps between the bodies and body parts takes most of her focus, but she still tries to keep an ear out for anything moving ahead of them.

They still haven't seen any sign of anything alive, and Penelope's not sure if she's glad for that or not.

For a moment, Penelope wished she knew how many people were on the ship. Or how many people were left on the ship?

How many bodies they'd have to see before this was all over with.

Teagan and Courtney stay close to her, both as they can be. They all walk so carefully, minimizing their sound. But they're sticking so close to her that Penelope can feel the heat off their bodies and the brush of limbs while walking as they try to step where she's been without waiting for her to be all the way out of the spot.

But there's just... No one.

No one alive.

Nothing down here with them.

They're not the first people there. They couldn't be. The bodies alone are sign enough of that, but Penelope wouldn't, couldn't, look at them long enough to check if they're passengers or crew.

Penelope calls out, calling for crew, calling for passengers, calling for anyone who might hear her.

It startles one of the others—she's not sure which—but she hears them thump heavily behind her. Penelope doesn't check, freezing to listen for signs of life around them.

But there's nothing.

Nothing at all.

Sure, someone might be in there and hiding from them, but Penelope gets the feeling that they're just...

Completely alone.

Completely, and totally, alone.

Creeping along further, they stumble across the kitchens. It doesn't feel like they find them intentionally. One second, they're lost, and the next, they're facing rooms that should be full of bustling people.

They're more extensive than Penelope thought, and she wonders how many people are supposed to be in there.

So much food is strewn around. Food that might have been safe to eat at one point left rotting on the floor. The fridges cracked open, freezing the room and leaving everything achingly cold.

It's been a two-week cruise in Alaska, and this is the first time that Penelope feels properly cold. The cold bites across her nose, cheeks, and hands.

It shocks her a bit, almost back to herself.

It's real, and she, Penelope, is here on this far too quiet ship. Or maybe it's just the kitchen—which feels like it should be full of bustle, noise, and people—is too quiet.

Penelope calls even as she walks through the kitchens, looking for anyone to answer, listening for any noise that might be from someone other than their little group.

It's more of a series of rooms, forcing them to spread out. Penelope spots Courtney eating something she'd grabbed, and her stomach clenches, reminding her that they were here for food first. Everything else could and would wait.

Some food seems to be safe to eat. Bread with a hell of a crust, other foods that might be safe. Penelope stays away from all the meat. Anything that's been out this long isn't safe. And maybe, just a little worried that she wouldn't be able to tell the pork or cow from... well, people.

Penelope hears soft sobbing while seeing if she can make the food she finds into something worth eating.

Teagan appears next to her, tapping Penelope on the shoulder and pointing toward the source, then her ear; Penelope nods, waving Courtney over to confirm she hears it, too.

They look at each other, wondering if getting involved is a good idea. But that isn't as important as the fact that they've found someone.

The sound is coming from a storage room off the central kitchen.

Inside, a man hunches over a body, crying.

More crying, more soul-wrenching, fully body-shaking sobs as he curls over a body on the ground, too still to be anything else.

Teagan, Courtney, and Penelope exchange looks.

Another silent bout of communication passes between them as they figure out what to do and whether they should approach.

Teagan steps forward, ignoring Penelope and Courtney, who are trying to pull her back. She slips away until she's just a few feet from the man.

Penelope tries to signal her back with big but silent gestures.

Her movements catch Teagan's eye, but she doesn't come back. She wants to check on the man. The heartbroken, heart-wrenching sobs are painful to hear, tugging at the heart.

Penelope wonders who the body was to him and stops trying to stop

Teagan.

Teagan inches closer and tries, "Sir?"

Penelope freezes, but if the man hears Teagan, he doesn't respond.

Moving a little closer, Teagan asks again, "Sir?"

Still, the man doesn't notice her. Teagan looks back at the others.

There's something wrong here.

She feels it, Penelope feels it, and she's sure Courtney feels it. Penelope wants to tell her to give up, to come back to them and back where it's safe. But even though Teagan appears just as uncomfortable, she keeps moving closer.

"Sir?" Teagan asks again, standing right behind him now. It doesn't seem like she's saying it any louder, but it feels like she's shouting.

Penelope wants nothing more than to drag her friend away. She doesn't know what's triggering the feeling, and she doesn't want to know. Not anymore. Now, she just wants to get her friend away from that man.

She knows she needs to; something deep inside her—a primal part of her—knows that there's something wrong here.

But she doesn't know how to say it or tell Teagan to get away from him and away from the danger Penelope immediately and deeply recognizes.

Despite everything Penelope is feeling, Teagan leans over and taps his shoulder.

The man turns and springs in a single, fluid movement.

Teagan's knocked to the floor, the man on top of her, his hands reaching for her throat.

He's gone from piteously weeping to screaming rage, forcing her to the ground.

Now, they can see the mess on his shirt, the gore in his teeth, the blood—and worse—stuck to his face.

The flip throws the form, revealing the cavernous wreck of a body ripped open from throat to groin.

He snaps his teeth at Teagan, pressing closer to her, his snapping jaws already too close to her and his hands scratching everything in reach.

Penelope finally moves.

Teagan tries to hold him away, screaming like a banshee, like a stuck pig, like a Nazgul, like every idiom Penelope has ever heard, never wondered about.

Penelope slams her makeshift club into his head—Courtney was only a second behind her—wishing she didn't know what Teagan's screams sounded like.

She's not trying to kill him; she just wants him away from her friends. She just wants him to stop making that terrifying noise.

Penelope doesn't want to kill him.

But he won't stop. He just won't stop.

Every time she hits him out, a pained, half-snarl escapes him.

Teagan is his only focus in the world.

Why didn't he stop? Why wouldn't he get off her?

It's a brutal way to die, the slam of clubs into him again and again. Penelope quickly loses track, giving in to the panic, fear, and adrenaline.

Finally, he stops snarling, stops screaming, stops moving.

Teagan shoves him off, still screaming as they pull her away, covered in so much blood.

Her own blood, the body's, the man's, it's impossible to tell.

She doesn't stay away for long, standing as soon as she can kick the body.

Penelope thinks it's just because she can. It must be if she's feeling anything like Penelope's feeling.

Penelope's horrified at their actions, aware on some level that she's just beaten a man to death.

But there was something really, really wrong here. Even if there wasn't, normal people don't attack others like that and don't eat people like that.

Teagan finally stumbles back, Courtney catching her.

Penelope needs to know. She needs to look at the man and see if she can figure out what's wrong with him.

Dark veins cross his face from an infected gouge in his jaw, all of it creeping down his neck.

The gouge on his face... looks like a bite mark.

"Oh shit," Courtney mutters behind her, "Oh no, this is really bad, we got to get her some help."

Turning around, Penelope can see Teagan's arms are bleeding badly, blood actively dripping to the floor. It's so bright and stands out so much more than the dried dark blood they've been seeing.

"Look around for something, anything we can use to wrap the wounds. We've got to get them covered." Penelope starts looking for a first aid kit or anything halfway sanitary.

Courtney finds where it's supposed to be, but the metal brackets usually holding it are severely damaged, like it was yanked off with great force.

She tells Penelope she's looking around for another kit, but Penelope finds a pile of clean, cloth napkins in the central kitchen. Thank God for fancy cruise ships.

Penelope's not a doctor; she has no idea what she's doing, and Teagan's fading too fast to tell her what to do. Wrapping Teagan's arms tightly, Penelope hopes she's covering the worst.

They'll figure out something better soon.

Courtney hears something in the hallway and signals Penelope to come with her.

Other people are in the halls for the first time in so many days. Courtney almost calls for help, but Penelope stops her, noticing the blood all over them.

They're wandering the halls, more than wandering, looking, almost investigating, with more following behind.

Suddenly, they're everywhere.

They have to hide. There are too many to get away, and they're blocking off the main pathway and getting closer.

Penelope looks around; what's their best bet?

Maybe locking themselves in the freezers?

12

Chapter 12

After what felt like hours, the scrabbling noises outside of the icy, freezing fridge finally stopped.

Just silence, again, the silence.

The girls huddled together in the fridge, trying to preserve their warmth as much as possible in the icy room. Penelope had flipped over plastic milk crates so they'd have something other than the icy metal to sit on. Around them, the food was too cold to eat, too cold at least while they were unable to warm it, unable to warm themselves.

Even though the noises died down quickly enough, they didn't open the doors immediately, knowing there was a chance there might still be some of the... some of the people outside.

Even though it's freezing.

Even though they don't really have the layers to spare, they wait.

Even though Courtney and Penelope give up their shirts to wrap Teagan's wounds as best they can, trying to stem the bleeding, they wait longer.

Waiting for any sign of the- people out in the kitchen still.

Teagan whimpers softly. She doesn't mean to, and the others don't try to keep her quiet. She was quiet enough, and any noises they might make to get her to stop were going to be louder.

Anyone, anything outside the doors, probably wouldn't hear her anyway.

Penelope looked over her wounds, checking if she'd bled through the second layer added by Courtney and Penelope's shirts. The wounds aren't clean; the meat of her arms looks like, well, meat.

But their makeshift wrappings are better than nothing. Better than the cloth napkins she'd already bled through. The red passes through the shirts as Teagan bleeds through those, too. Penelope doesn't say anything; she just catches Courtney's eyes. They know they have to do something, and fast.

They figure out what they're going to do in mutters and rough hand signs, eventually settling on something like a plan.

Counting down silently, Penelope and Courtney creep out.

A few of the people, sick people (though, were they still actually, really, people?), are in the kitchen. A couple stumble around, still following after the group, and a couple more are just leaning on the counters, the workstations—not really moving, not following, not even looking around, just leaning.

They've got to deal with them, though, even if they're apparently distracted.

It makes her sick to think about killing off the remaining ones; it seems cruel. Whatever's wrong with them isn't their fault.

But now wasn't the time.

The few who weren't just leaning eventually wandered off after the rest of the... people went off.

This time, Penelope and Courtney sneak up on them. This time, with less worry about Teagan clouding their senses. This time, it really sticks just how hard it is to beat a man's head in.

It makes Penelope sick, and she's almost glad she hadn't eaten earlier. Though she hadn't had the chance.

It's a little easier when the second one turns toward her. When he- it reaches out, sputtering nonsense noises that are almost words; she thinks he's talking to her, but it's not actual words, at least nothing she recognizes.

Her shock is almost enough to get her killed, the man getting too close for her to hit him before she realizes.

Courtney saves her, acting faster than Penelope, slamming her makeshift club into his- its head.

It goes down.

Penelope looks at Courtney before rushing to get Teagan.

They've got to leave this portion of the ship. There's no telling when the group of people will be back, but they can't just lock themselves in the freezer again.

It'll kill them, quick.

It'd be a peaceful way to go, though.

Now, though, they need food to find out what's happening. Courtney and Penelope avoid making any noise while packing up a couple makeshift bags of food, anything that'll be easy to carry. Anything that's left, really.

There's not enough food, not enough for how long the rest of the cruise is supposed to be, but it's better than starving and waiting around some more.

They leave the kitchen and go back to the darker halls, which are enclosed and have a small feeling of the crew-only portions of the ships. Looking for any signs of anything in the dim halls with them, but it's hard to keep an eye out while trying to stay as quiet and juggle Teagan in shock. She's not at her best; she needs more help than they can give. They can't exactly call out for anyone, not knowing if there's going to be someone—something—around the corner for them.

"How do we figure out what we need to do next?" Courtney asks, voice low.

"We know what we're going to do next. We're going to figure out how to get to the infirmary."

"But how are we going to get there?"

Weighed down by Teagan, Penelope feels like she's trying to explain this to a toddler. "We're gonna find a map and then try to take the most direct route."

"Don't talk to me like I'm a kid."

"I'm not-" Okay, she is, but, "-there's no better way to describe it. We can figure out more of what to do from there. But for now, we gotta get to the infirmary for Teagan's sake."

"Right." Courtney pauses, looking at Teagan, "You're right, we've gotta go."

Sneaking along is much harder with Teagan, not all there, and slower as they head back toward the area where Penelope thinks the infirmary is. It would at least keep them on something like the right path, going the right way. That it happens to be in the opposite direction from where the others had gone was pure chance.

Courtney focuses on taking pictures. She says it's so they know where they've been, where they're going, but Penelope's pretty sure it's so she'll have some 'behind the scenes' pictures when they get home.

Penelope hopes they don't get killed for one of her pictures as they creep along.

The pictures she takes leaning around corners, looking for any sign of the things, are very helpful, though. They make getting around a bit easier.

But that's how they run into Charlie, though it's more like he runs into them. Darting around a corner, he nearly hits Courtney with his knife while she's distracted, taking a picture of something less important but still 'behind the scenes.'

"Who are you?" Charlie asks as soon as he realizes they're real people, not the not people.

"I'm Penelope," she introduces herself, hefting Teagan a little higher. He looks familiar; Penelope's sure she's seen him before. "This is Teagan, and the woman you almost ran into is Courtney. Who are you?"

"I'm Charlie."

"Where are your parents, Charlie?" Teagan slurs, mother henning even though she's in no state to.

"I've been on the cruise with a friend's family. They didn't pay much attention to me-" Charlie shrugs, "-so long as I didn't cost them more money and didn't get them in trouble too, they didn't care."

"Why aren't you with them now though?"

"I snuck back here as soon as I was able to; the outer decks have been a complete shitshow-"

"Language." Courtney cuts him off.

"Is now really the time, lady?" The kid snaps. "If you've got a better word for it, I'd love to hear it."

"I'd call it a massacre. There's no telling how many people died out there."

Charlie huffs a laugh, "Yeah, and they're all over the ship. At least here, the zoms don't notice you if you're quiet. I think their eyes are too messed up to see right down here."

"Zoms?" Penelope asks, though she already knows.

"You know, the fucking zombies that have overtaken the whole ship?" Charlie's voice is rising, getting louder, and she knows they're not being very understanding, but he's gotta quiet down.

Even though Penelope knows it's a bad idea, she shushes him, "Please. You're right about them being interested in sound, so please!"

Charlie freezes.

Penelope looks him over; he's got lots of blood and other stuff that she doesn't want to identify dried on his clothes. It doesn't look like he's injured, though. He's clutching a steak knife with both hands, and Penelope can only imagine the damage he can inflict.

"Where'd you get the knife?

"I stole it. Got it from the dinner table pretty early on. I don't like that they took all our stuff when we got on board. I just said I wasn't feeling well, and my friend's family didn't even seem to notice."

"How have you been avoiding..." Penelope doesn't want to say 'Zoms,' or zombies, or anything that might make this more real.

"I've mostly been squeezing myself in the cupboards and stuff when I see too many of 'em." He rubs his arm, "Any, really, of them. I can take one of them if they're lying down or distracted, but not if there's more."

He shakes his head, and Penelope can only imagine what he's seen. They've only been out of their own room for an hour or maybe two, and they've already seen some terrible things.

The first man's heartbroken sobs flash through her mind.

They've already done terrible things.

Penelope closes her eyes, forcing the thought away, "You want to come with us? We're going to the infirmary."

"Uh, sure, I think it might be easier to go around, though." Charlie pauses, "And you'll all have to be quieter. You're too loud. You'll get us killed."

"We'll do our best," Teagan says with a tight smile, muffling most of her pained sounds.

"I more meant that one." Charlie points at Courtney, who's still taking pictures.

"She'll do her best too, we promise," Penelope says, wanting to keep this kid from going off alone and getting killed.

Not that they were doing better.

13

Chapter 13

Something was itching at her—the little place at the back of her brain that wanted to know things, that wanted to take things apart and see how they worked.

They were on a cruise ship vacation, so it should have been pretty safe, all things considered. Maybe there was a slightly higher chance than usual of catching something. Still, they were all sharing breathing and communal living spaces. Diseases spread like wildfires in those kinds of environments.

Penelope and the others hadn't spent much time in the communal areas. Penelope hadn't; she'd gotten off the ship every chance she got, and she'd been hiding away in the cabin whenever she wasn't out and about. The closest she'd gotten was dinner every night and going to the casino that last night.

They really should have noticed this before it happened. Someone should have noticed something, maybe even someone in their group. Something like people tearing each other to shreds should have been caught by someone. There had to be warnings, or warning signs at least, before they just locked everyone in their rooms and functionally threw away the keys. People acted out of the norm before they started killing each other before they turned into mindless monsters.

Then again, who would be able to tell if people were acting out of the norm?

Penelope loved her friends and knew them pretty well. Still, it would be impossible to tell if Melissa was acting oddly for most of the trip because she'd been all over the place, all over the towns, on different excursions, focusing so hard on getting out there and getting photos for her socials. Penelope hadn't even known where she was most of that time, and when they did cross paths, it was usually for so little time that they just caught up as quick as possible before going on to their next thing.

Teagan had been pretty normal this trip; she'd spent most of it on the phone with Colby, but if she'd been off the phone, would it have made it easier for Penelope to notice something was wrong? Would her worry about not constantly being in contact with Colby be out of character for her? Or would it be weirder if she wasn't trying to get in contact with him?

Courtney was acting out of character, taking all the pictures, but that was just who she was on vacation and trying not to get bogged down by her breakup.

Would they notice if Penelope was acting out of character?

Would she notice if she was?

How far would it go?

"We should try to find out what happened," Penelope tells the others. She knows now's not the time, but she's got to focus on literally anything other than Teagan bleeding out when they're moving as fast as they can. Would you guys be willing to help me look for anything that might help us figure out what happened?"

"Do you think now is the time for that?" Teagan asks, her hands shaking heavily. Penelope can't tell if it's from blood loss, cold, or something else.

They're still moving along; the infirmary is their main goal now, but they'll need to get off the ship somehow eventually, "If we find out what it is, where it started, we might be able to help-"

She wants to say others, she wants to say the people who've been infected by whatever this is, she wants to say something that sounds like it'll actually do anything.

"We might be able to help someone."

"Penelope-" Courtney starts, probably telling her that it's stupid, a bad plan, or just going to get them all killed, but then Charlie cuts them off.

"Hey! Maybe there'll be a first aid kit or something if we go to the rally points."

"That's a good idea," Teagan tells him, and Penelope can hear the none-too-subtle, and Penelope's idea isn't very good.

She just wanted to know how the ship got overrun, why it got overrun, and what was going on. If they knew, it might be something they could pass on to, like, the CDC, to other survivors. If there were any other survivors. "Yeah, and if there's still a life vessel, we might just be able to get off of here instead."

Charlie leads the way. He remembers where he was supposed to go for his own rally, and though it's not the one that the girls were supposed to go to, it was a plan, at least.

And it was better than getting lost in the depths of the ship. Again.

Penelope wonders where the signs all are. They're supposed to be all over the place, so they have to find one eventually, but Penelope doesn't see any of them. Each time she tries to point a way out of the back, it's the wrong way. It seems like every choice she makes seems to be the wrong one, at least as far as directions.

To get to Charlie's rally point, they have to leave the enclosed halls for the open parts of the ship.

Now, sneaking past all the open areas makes Penelope's skin prickle, her hair rising at the risk of threat unseen. Her head swivels as she looks around for anything out of place. Thinking for a moment, she sees something out of the corner of her eye, though nothing is there when she turns to look. People could be around any corner, anywhere, and they wouldn't know it until it was too late.

There isn't anywhere for them to hide if they need to.

Soon, though not soon enough, or maybe too soon, they're opening the doors to the rally point.

Penelope covers her mouth out of shock or reflex she doesn't know. But she can't focus on anything but the smell.

The smell of blood so thick lays across her tongue, and the hint of rot underneath it is strong, even with the wind sweeping it away.

It doesn't matter if she covers her mouth and nose or not.

It's sinking into her, becoming part of her.

The once gray deck is red with blood, so much of it it's hard to walk without slipping.

Bodies and body parts are spread across the deck, and Penelope fights the urge to look too closely, hoping beyond hope she doesn't recognize anyone.

Oh God.

They don't have time to gawp, though. There are more people in front of them—only a couple, fortunately—but they don't have time to focus on the bloodbath. They have to defend themselves now.

Penelope shakes her head, looking at the mess on the ground and trying not to throw up.

An older woman stumbles toward Penelope, but she can't think or focus.

She couldn't think about who this woman was, her life, her family, or her favorite meal.

She just needs to deal with her.

With it.

Penelope barely manages to keep herself in check, but only barely.

It's more than the smell of blood making her sick, lingering every-where, completely unavoidable. It's worse than before, worse than inside, it didn't seem possible, but it was so much worse.

When she looks around, Courtney's already dealt with one stumbling over to her and has started taking pictures of them, looking for identifiable features and taking pictures of their faces.

Penelope couldn't watch. Nausea rolled through her at just the thought.

She just couldn't.

"It's there," Teagan calls out, startlingly loud.

"What?" Penelope tries to keep her voice down.

"Over there," she points to Penelope's left, "The first aid kit."

And there it is. Glaringly obvious and covered in no small amount of blood.

She walks Teagan to a bench before retrieving the first aid kit. There aren't any good places to set it down, but she settles on a spot that looks cleaner than the rest. Thankfully, it seems fully stocked, and despite the blood everywhere, the kit's interior is clean.

Penelope isn't, though; she doesn't know if it's safe for her to try to provide care like this.

She hesitates to touch anything at all, not even Teagan.

The hands grabbing hers give her pause, and she looks up to see that it's Courtney holding them. "How about I do that, okay?"

Penelope nods and pulls her hands back.

It's only then that she realizes how much she's shaking. She hadn't felt it, hadn't realized it.

It only takes a few seconds of watching Courtney unwrap the bandages to decide she's going to look around for a bit. Courtney's capable, at least, more capable than Penelope right now, and if watching her rewrap Teagan's arms is too much, then maybe doing anything else would help.

Penelope leans over the edge of the boat; she's gasping for air; when did that start? She tries to even her breathing, focusing on anything but the smell around her, the slight squish under her shoes.

Even though it was still pouring rain, it wasn't enough to wash away the smell; this deck was covered like their balcony had been.

Courtney calls her over to look at Teagan's wounds. They're not looking any better than they were. If anything, they look worse now that they can see the damage without all the blood. There's still blood leaking sluggishly, and removing the makeshift bandages opened some of the wounds, but it's not as bad as it was. The skin now looks puffy, but it doesn't look inflamed.

Teagan is still too pale, but she says it's pretty normal, given that she hasn't taken anti-inflammatories. She doesn't think they're infected.

Penelope points out they don't appear to have any black lines like the others, but that's all she can manage before her stomach starts rolling again.

Charlie calls for her next. He refuses to look at Teagan's arms and looks about as green in the face as Penelope feels.

All the lifeboats on this side of the ship have all been launched.

There's still a chance there are lifeboats, or there might be another way off, but they're not getting off this ship right now.

And worse, there's more infected here than they thought.

There's a lot of blood and viscera, but the two infected they'd found up here wouldn't have been able to manage all this.

There have to be more infected here than they've seen because there's no way they managed all this damage on their own. The blood makes it hard to tell exactly how many; given how much of it there is, it could be more. And she doesn't know how much of the blood spilled is still there or how much of the bodies that were shredded were dropped off the edge or taken somewhere else. She's pretty sure there's evidence of at least a dozen people here.

Some of the bodies she can quickly identify as- as the- as infected. Almost all of them have bite wounds with black lines radiating from them. Some are fainter than others, but the lines are obviously there.

But some other bodies have lines that don't look as severe or inflamed as the ones on the more dangerously infected.

She wonders what it is and how they got it.

The bite wounds are obvious; if the lines aren't infected themselves, they're a surefire indicator of it.

On the other hand, the scratches didn't look to be from hands. Some of them just looked like deep gouges.

Maybe it didn't have to be by bites?

Or is it saliva-based, and these were infected after being hurt?

It didn't matter now; it wasn't important.

They just need to ensure they keep all wounds covered and far enough away to avoid getting bit.

However, that was easier said than done.

As much as the deep, encompassing rage flows through Penelope at being left behind, she hopes they get to shore safely. She hopes they send help, that it's already on the way.

She hopes they just have to wait.

They can wait a little longer.

... — — — ... ... — — — ... ... — — — ...

Penelope feels the hands grasp her shoulders hard. It's surprising, it hurts.

At first, she thinks it's Courtney or the kid. Maybe they got scared or something? She tries to turn, but then Courtney is there—actually there now.

Between her and the man scratching at both of them.

She nearly screams, realizing it's so close to her, but the sound gets caught in her throat.

Painful and stuck.

Now isn't the time, and screaming won't help when more of them are coming from nowhere.

In a flurry, so fast she almost misses it, they're out and scratching, gargling, making such godawful noises, she thinks she can even hear the one closest to her apologize, but that can't be right.

That can't be right.

That can't be right.

She swings at the other one; she's hurt, but not bit. It's a miracle. She'd felt its breath on her; she'd thought it was Courtney.

She'd thought she was safe.

She body slams one of them away from Courtney, swinging wildly, just trying to get them off, get them away, get them to stop.

And then it's over, all over. They're dead or on the ground.

Charlie falls onto the last one to stab it in the head.

They're dead. Dead, dead, dead.

Teagan is okay; she hadn't had a chance to stand up, let alone get more hurt. Penelope thinks she's okay; the adrenaline rushing through her makes it hard to tell.

Courtney, though, had taken the worst of it in trying to protect Penelope.

She grabs the first aid kit, trying to figure out the worst damage and where to start.

A deep scratch on her face bleeds sluggishly. Head wounds always bleed a lot, but it probably wasn't the most important.

There are more severe ones, heavily bleeding wounds on her neck and chest. She looked damn near flayed open, and all of them were weeping blood steadily.

The first aid kit doesn't have enough to deal with all the damage.

Pressing sterile pads against as much as she could, Penelope was deeply, deeply aware they didn't have enough supplies, and now their shirts were covered with blood, worse, and had the potential to carry whatever the hell this virus was.

They need to do something.

Charlie is freaking out, it takes Penelope a minute to realize, but she needs him calm, calmer, at least.

But he'd killed his first Z, his first human, and he continued freaking out about it.

Penelope understood: "I understand. God, I understood so much, Charlie, okay? I know that you're scared and horrified, but I need you to focus, okay? I need you to help me, help Courtney and Teaganokay, okay?"

"But I-"

"I know, Charlie. But Courtney and Teagan are both hurt bad, and we don't know if there's more of those on their way."

"I don't-"

"You need to help us get to the infirmary, okay?" Penelope's hands are covered in too much blood, and Courtney's quickly losing focus, possibly losing consciousness. How was she fading so much faster than Teagan had? "Look, I don't know if Courtney is going to be conscious for much longer, and I don't think I'll be able to move her if she passes out. Teagan's in no place to help me either, so I need you to help us, okay?"

"I don't know if I can-"

"You've gotta, Charlie. After all, you've explored so much of the ship, right? Right?" Charlie nods, "You should know. You've explored so much more of the ship than any of us, so you're probably able to get around a lot better than any of us. We don't know where we're going, and we need you right now."

Charlie nods, "Okay. Okay. I think I know where we need to go, but..."

"But what?" He hesitates, "Please, we need to get moving. This is not a safe space for us."

"I'm not sure it'll be safe to get there." Charlie looks up at her imploringly, like he's hoping for anything else.

"It's a risk we're going to have to take."

14

Chapter 14

Time seems to creep by at a crawl as they head to the infirmary again. This time, they have no choice but to get there; their need is too high to be dealt with by a first aid kit alone.

Courtney rallies, but not enough, and it's only enough to keep her moving forward. Penelope has to support most of her weight through the ship, and Teagan props her up on the other side as best she can in her own state.

Teagan holds Courtney's club, but it's the most she can do. They all know she won't be able to fight with it, even if it comes to the worst.

Charlie leads them along, though he's jumping at every noise now, his earlier quiet bravado completely broken by the appearance of the- of their attackers and his own hand in their deaths.

They reach the infirmary after far too long spent creeping through the ship. Penelope is most surprised by the complete lack of resistance.

A little luck for once, probably the only time in this mess.

It is not as bad as Penelope anticipated; she'd thought it would be just as much of a bloodbath as the rally point.

They find some mess, but not as bad or nearly as much. Someone had obviously cleaned up at some point. The blood spatters on the walls were wiped down; not well, and obviously not with actual cleaners, but it was done. Things are still neatly placed on the tables and counters. No sign of people here now; they'd be able to see anyone else in the small space, but obviously, whoever had been here had cleaned up after themselves.

Setting Courtney down on one of the beds, Penelope turns to Teagan for guidance. Still, probably in shock, Teagan quietly guides Penelope through finding what they'd need and how to ensure they're sterile.

This area hasn't been as raided as the others. If it had been at all. Finding what Teagan figured she'd need to patch Courtney and herself back together was easy.

They couldn't have been more lucky. This place was fully stocked and practically untouched, and finding everything they needed and then some was a breeze with Charlie's help.

Teagan cleans up the wounds on Courtney's chest and neck, telling her they'll get her fixed up in no time. She's gentle even with her own shaking hands, probably glad for something to do, something to take her mind off her own pain.

As she focused on Courtney's, she told Charlie how to bandage Penelope's wounds, grumbling about how most places had plenty of extra hands, but she was forced to work alone here.

Penelope just let the words roll over her; she was pretty sure she was in shock again? Still? And wasn't dealing too well. Luckily for her, most of her wounds are superficial, and none show any sign of the bleeding black veins.

She insists on checking Teagan for any signs, too. Teagan has a low-grade fever, but there's no sign of infection in the wounds; though it's only been a couple of hours since the first attack, Penelope wants to take that as a good sign.

Another lucky break is the bank of painkillers in the infirmary, and they manage to go a long way, too, though Penelope chooses to take some aspirin. She doesn't want to potentially dull her mind, and even if she weren't still shocked, she doesn't think she feels any pain.

She feels like she's not doing enough.

... — — — ... ... — — — ... ... — — — ...

The other settled down slowly. There aren't any windows, which at least gives the comfort of nothing being able to come through one of them, but it's too still. Now, there's nothing outside but nothing they can see.

But there was no telling how long that would be true.

Penelope gets up and walks around while the others try to rest. She thinks locking the door and barricading it will make it feel a little safer, at least giving them more warning if something tries to get through.

The medical center isn't big, but there are enough beds for everyone to curl up and at least try to sleep. Penelope probably could, too, if she wanted, and there's an examining table that honestly doesn't look too uncomfortable.

But she's not ready to try yet, and even if she were ready, she's not sure that it would be safe for them all to sleep at the same time.

Charlie was already conked. Apparently, kids could sleep anywhere. And given the kind of day she knew the poor kid had had, she wasn't too surprised.

They also didn't know how long he'd been awake. If he'd gotten much sleep in the days leading up to their meeting, to him guiding them all around. He was a good kid and had been a big help so far, but he was still just a kid. Penelope didn't know how old he was, but she thought that he might be in his early teens. Though the long, thin limbs might trick your guess, he had a baby face and wasn't terribly sure about most of his actions.

Teagan was tossing and turning, though, not asleep but obviously trying to.

"You should dose yourself with something stronger." She tells the other, quiet, to avoid waking Courtney and the kid, who had already been dosed with something a little stronger.

"I need to be alert," Teagan argues without hesitation.

"You need to sleep. And you're not going to sleep if you don't take anything to help with the pain." Penelope insists.

"It's not safe enough to sleep too deep here. I don't even like that I had to give Courtney something."

Penelope looks at where Courtney is sleeping like a corpse, arms crossed over her belly. "She needed it. You both need to heal, and you're not going to do that if you're not sleeping. And if you keep jostling your wounds, they're just going to take longer to heal."

"I thought I was the nurse here," Teagan grumbles, sitting up.

Penelope smiles, offering a hand to help Teagan, "What's the saying? Even the carer needs caring?"

"That's a stupid quote," Teagan says, exhaustion coloring her voice.

After some more reluctance and after checking the door herself, Teagan makes Penelope promise. "You have to wake me up if something, anything happens. Okay?"

Penelope agrees, just trying to get her to actually sleep, "I promise."

"Say it to me; tell me you'll wake me up." Teagan's scared; it's a new look on her Penelope.

"I promise, Teagan, I'll wake you up. If anything at all happens, you'll be the first to know, other than me."

"Okay." Teagan nods and gives herself a smaller dose of something than she'd given Courtney.

Once she's sure that Teagan is actually sleeping, Penelope starts poking around, looking for something, anything to waste the time.

She's not even sure what she's looking for. There's probably just going to be people's medical nonsense in here and maybe some notes or something about one or another thing that the doctor, or whatever they had on the ship, was interested in.

Nothing was very interesting here.

Sitting at the desk eventually, Penelope's mostly just worn herself out. Not that she'd had a lot of energy anyway. There's not a lot in their bag of food, maybe enough for a meal or two for each of them. Grabbing just a small thing, just enough to maybe tide her over for a couple more hours, Penelope looks through some of the stuff on what's probably the doctor's desk.

And that's when she finds a notebook. It's completely innocuous, a single-subject notebook that wouldn't stand out anywhere, but it catches her eye.

Maybe because it's perfectly normal, and its perfectly normal nature seems to be completely at odds with everything else from the last few days.

There's nothing worth paying attention to in the first few pages. It seems it's the doctor's handy book, something they drop all their thoughts into to parcel out later. But about halfway in are the notes from this last week. With various notes about the last week being perfectly normal, Penelope doesn't expect much.

Then, she found a log of what had happened with the first patient. Less actual log, more like the doctor was trying to put together what had happened in her own head. How he'd been feverish, his list of symptoms, they'd wanted to move him off the ship. Still, the captain had thought he'd be fine until they landed in Skagway, and the man had attacked a member of the crew and one of the nurses.

At that point, he was too much of a threat to keep on board. He'd been violent, stopped responding to questions, and was all around in the midst of some kind of crisis.

They'd kicked that guy off at the next port, along with his wife. The guy's wife was also symptomatic, but in different places and different ways; although the first patient had been bitten by someone, the wife didn't have any obvious signs of initial infection, just fever and the expression of her veins around her face and neck.

Unlike the first patient, though, she'd fallen into a coma-like state not long after coming to the infirmary with her husband the second time.

The ship didn't have the tools aboard to deal with those situations, so they'd opted to send her off as well, warning the receiving hospital that the husband had become incredibly violent and that they were unsure if she would come around with those symptoms.

The nurse had become symptomatic sooner than the other infected crewman; the doctor thought it might have had something to do with the location of the infection. The nurse and crewmen had been quarantined in the infirmary. Still, then the nurse attacked the other nurse who'd been sent to check on her, escaping and attacking multiple other crew and patients.

That's when the doctor suggested a ship-wide quarantine; they didn't know if other infected persons were on the ship.

Though the nurse and crewman were believed to be the first, they couldn't be certain if the husband hadn't somehow infected others like his wife had been, with no obvious outward indication of infection.

But the other infected people acted erratically and then attacked their fellow crew and passengers who'd left their quarters against instruction.

The final notes in the notebook were about the doctors themselves being attacked and locking themselves in the infirmary. They hadn't let anyone else into the room at that time, both their nurses already infected, and without any support, they knew it was only a matter of time until whatever the virus was had run its course, either, and they dropped into a coma or turned into a raging, gibbering monster.

They kept track of their symptoms, fever, and even the spread of the black veins from the bite wound on their hand, charting the growth of the veins.

They did that for almost two days based on the timeline they kept in the notes, and then from there, the notes changed; they started talking about things that pissed them off and scared them more until they turned into meaningless scribbles, a few things cut Penelope through, in the midst of some psycho-babble as an apology to their family, to their mom for dodging her calls, and for not coming home for Christmas the year before.

Penelope wondered how long it would be before they'd lost their minds. The timeline of the other part was very in-depth, but after the scribbles started, there was no telling, like their only solace was in writing.

Penelope wondered where they went. Did they leave the infirmary willingly? Did someone let them out?

It didn't matter.

They were gone, probably functionally dead. And this was here now.

At least she knew the symptoms now, from their reports and notes. If Teagan wasn't already showing some symptoms, she would probably be safe from whatever turned the others into an infection. She'd need to keep an eye on Courtney's wounds; the virus could be spread through spit if it landed in an open wound, and with her chest torn open like that, there was no telling for sure if she'd gotten it.

But now, all of them had open wounds. All of them were at risk of infection.

Well, not the kid, but he was another thing entirely.

Penelope would check Courtney's wounds herself in the morning or whenever the others were awake again. Even with the bloody mess she was, Penelope was sure that the veins would still be obvious.

15

Chapter 15

Penelope lay on the small cot with Charlie, petting his back and letting him cry.

He'd started sniffling and whimpering sometime after she'd finished reading the notebook and done a couple more laps of the room. Though it wasn't something she was comfortable with, she'd tried to wake him up. He'd swung his knife around like a crazy person until he'd recognized where he was.

Then he'd burst into tears, nearly silent, just a stuttered inhale barely audible.

Penelope didn't say a word; crawling into the too-small bed with him and holding him. God knew she needed human contact right now, and she wasn't about to keep this kid from it.

Since his sobs had nearly completely quieted, and his breathing was mostly evening out, Penelope was thinking about getting up and looking around a little more. Or she would have if he wasn't using her arm as a pillow.

It hadn't been long enough for them to get enough sleep, and the others needed it. Penelope needed to keep moving and watch, or she'd fall asleep. She couldn't sleep yet; it wasn't safe. When someone else had gotten enough sleep, she'd get some rest.

Her eyelids still fluttered under their weight, and she was pretty comfortable. Having a soft, warm body in her arms, one releasing a ton of sleepy heat, wasn't helping either. She needed to stay awake a little longer, though, at least until someone else woke up enough for her to get some sleep.

Hard knocks, cop knocks, slam against the door, pulling Penelope from the edge of sleep.

Then heavier, slightly further apart knocks, like something's being slammed into the door with each dull thud.

The noise wakes them all up. Teagan and Courtney look at Penelope and each other, trying to decide whether to open the doors.

Then metallic clangs, like something metal is being hit against the outside. It's impossible to tell what's making the noise, but Penelope knows that whatever's making all that noise is probably going to bring all the infected right to this door.

From what she's read, Penelope thinks they wouldn't think to use weapons against the doors, but she's very sure that they should be, need to be ready to leave right now.

And if there are no infected, if it's people who are trying to rescue them, then they still need to get out of here just in case all the noise draws the zombies right to the door.

Teagan and Charlie rush to pack up things; Charlie has space in his backpack, and Teagan is more about guessing what they'd need from this room than anyone else.

Courtney and Penelope move stuff out of the way to open the doors themselves. Even if there's infected outside, they need to get out of here, and they'll need to do it fast.

This place is closed off, without a second escape route.

If they get trapped here, they'll be really, really trapped.

After a couple of minutes, the sounds mostly drop to a scrabbling noise. Penelope thinks whoever's out there is likely realizing the doors were secured shut in some way and might be trying to get the doors off the hinges.

Because that was the only downside of the doors opening outward here.

Penelope starts counting down to Courtney, not wanting to take the chance if they're wrong and it is infected outside.

Then, she kicks the door open.

...— — —... ...— — —... ...— — —...

Even though it was probably the noisiest option, it was better to kick it open and catch whoever was out there off guard.

It would give them more time to get out of there.

Instead, Neil, of all people, gets knocked back by the door, and the meaty thunk of it hits him sickeningly.

Hitting Neil specifically hadn't been the plan. Still, it works as well as anything else Penelope could have tried—better, even some might say, given that it distracts everyone.

The people on the other side of the door are Melissa and Brody, who falter as they jump forward, raising their own makeshift weapons.

But Melissa recognizes them, running to Penelope for a hug.

She's babbling immediately, and it takes Penelope a second to figure out what she's saying, "I'm so glad it's you and not something scary, Oh, I was so scared. I didn't know what'd happened to you guys or if you'd left without me. I didn't think you would, but I didn't know!"

"It's okay, it's okay," Penelope pats her back, trying to make eye contact with Teagan and Courtney. "I'm glad you're okay. We didn't know what happened to you!"

"We've been in Brody's room. We thought it would just blow over!"

"Why were you banging on the door like that? You had to know that it was a bad idea, that it would attract more of the-"

"We know we're being followed!" Melissa turns around, looking behind them. "We're pretty sure they're far enough away that we could hide here!"

"Then why were you banging on the door?" Penelope wants to shake her, but she has too much self-control.

"We just gotta hide. It'll be safer in there, right?"

Penelope holds back a scream of frustration, "Not since you made all that racket; they probably know where we are! We gotta move!"

The other three have backpacks, which is miles better than carrying everything and hoping they didn't drop it. She snags Melissa's backpack, pulling it open so the others can dump what they can into the bags.

"But the doors were so hard to get into," Melissa says plaintively.

Penelope huffs; there's so much she could say that she wants to say, but none of it will help. She needs to think.

They'd spent so much time making so much noise, and Penelope didn't know how far the infected were behind them or if they'd have time to get away.

But, they also need to check for signs of infection, "Were any of you bit? Or scratched?"

"What?"

"Were you bit or scratched?" Penelope screeches. It's not helpful, but she can hear the- others down the hall. They're already coming. They've already lost too much valuable time to get away. "Have any of you been infected by them?"

"No, I don't think so," Melissa says Brody shows a long, painful-looking mark going from his neck down his chest, but it doesn't look infected—at least not infected by the mystery disease.

"Nah, they couldn't catch me if they tried," Neil says, full of bravado.

"Good," The noises are getting louder, half gibbering, half words, half something else, "We have to go right now."

"What? But the infirmary is right there; that's gotta be a million times better than running around the ship!" Melissa argues.

"It would be if you guys hadn't made so much noise!" Teagan hushes her.

Neil scoffs, "Come on, that's insane; those doors are super study. I had to take off the hinges to get them open."

"Yeah, and did you consider how long it would take to get them back on?" Penelope spits; they can't go out the way they came in.

"It wouldn't have taken that long." He whines, and Penelope wonders how Melissa and Brody didn't leave him somewhere already.

"Yes, it would have! You'd be dead, and so would we."

Melissa tugs on Penelope, "But- it's safer there."

"It would be if you hadn't brought a swarm of them down on us," Teagan tells her, zipping up the bag and shoving it back at Melissa. "They'd probably be able to get through those doors eventually just with sheer numbers."

"We're going to have to head deeper into the ship to get away," Penelope tells them. The infirmary is no longer safe, and I don't know where it's going to be."

"That was our best bet." Melissa whimpers.

"We gotta go; right now," she says, dragging Melissa down the hallway. At least Teagan and Courtney are already following. Charlie is all but glued to her side again.

They turn a corner to find that even if this new group wasn't followed by a swarm of gnashing teeth, there's a lot of them just all over the place. They're really everywhere.

"That way!" Charlie points, and the others follow without question; the number of infected is too much to question him.

There are more of them than Penelope thought possible. They had to run out eventually, right? There'd been a lot of people on the ship, but she'd thought for sure that there wouldn't be this many, or maybe that they'd stop at some point, or that more people had gotten off the ship before now.

But they just seemed to be everywhere, and all of them were coming towards their group now.

Was it possible for them to track their group somehow? Were they intentionally looking for them? Were these gnashing maws actually able to follow them over the sounds they made?

They needed to make as little noise as possible. But the now larger group can't move as silently as the smaller groups, and even if they could, they weren't trying to attack or draw them away.

And it seemed like they just kept showing up.

Every corner they took had more.

Inside, the ship wouldn't work; they were going to get killed in a dark hallway without a sign of where they were going.

"Alright, guys!" Penelope announces, not too worried about being quiet with everything around them, "If anyone knows if there's any way out of this section, now's the time!"

"Wait," Charlie answers, "I think there's a staircase just over that way that might get us out, but what if it's full of the zombies?"

"It's better than being trapped here with all of them. Lead the way, kid!" Penelope pushes him forward, with the others following her.

The mid-portion of the ship has a pathway that goes all the way around the ship; unfortunately, they can't launch the remaining lifeboats because the infected are too close behind them.

Hurrying as fast as they can, they end up nearly doing a lap of the ship before they manage to lose most of the infected.

They discover it by accident when Neil throws a soda can, which bursts explosively against the wall. It turns out it was that easy to find a good method to get rid of their followers. All they had to do was throw something, anything, really. As long as it's loud enough and keeps making noise, it would work to distract their pursuers so they can get away.

It's not a perfect method, and hearing all the noises of the infected as they near run is unsettling, but it works for long enough that they can get away again.

16

Chapter 16

It's a collective decision to find a place to sleep again; no one's well rested, and Penelope least of all. She didn't even know the last time she slept, and with the dark, looming cloud cover, it was hard to tell the time at a glance. After more discussion, they decide to hide away to sleep in one of the crew cabins.

As they creep down to the crew quarters, they expect to find infected around any and every corner, the echoes of shuffled footsteps and groans, grumbles, and sobs. But each time they round the corner, there's nothing and no one. Just more sounds from an unknown location.

Most of the lights down are off. Maybe it was intentional, maybe it was power issues, or maybe it was just that there weren't as many lights in this section.

It is harder to tell where the grumbling, groaning, and crying sounds are coming from and for them to move forward.

That had been a sticking point for all of them. Did they risk going in, where they'd be able to hear the infected so much easier, but where they'd be able to hear them too? Did they go to the parts of the ship where it was brighter but at more risk?

Did Penelope care about any of it more than her need for sleep right then? She can't even remember the last time she got to rest; every time she'd even sat down, she'd been doing something, freezing or first aid or comforting.

She dead on her feet- Well. Not dead, tired. So very, very tired.

It's dark there, so dark they have to shuffle along. Not that Penelope could do anything more intensive than that right now anyway, and she prays that they don't run into anything or anyone while in the halls. They can hear a few who are infected with them, but they don't seem to notice the still living—the people who aren't infected, that is—who are trying to avoid them.

They pass a few rooms, looking for something to hold them all, but that isn't possible. The crew section isn't exactly comfortable, but it's better than nothing, and at least there are multiple beds in some rooms.

Penelope hadn't realized how spacious their cabin was. She'd take back all previous complaints about being in each other's pockets.

That could wait, as they'd found a clean room that looked untouched.

She collapses into one of the beds, exhaustion already overtaking her as she drops. The room is tiny, but at least there are three bunks— nearly enough for everyone. And it's clean enough—clean's better than anything else, and there was no telling when she could rest again.

Penelope wonders who has the food; her stomach is eating itself. But she is also too tired to care about that now. That is a problem for later.

The others are keeping watch.

The room was away from most of the infected.

She can drift right off to sleep...

... — — ... ... — — ... ... — — ...

Then there's a lot of yelling, far, far too soon for anything but a few seconds to have passed.

She rockets herself up, trying to figure out what's going on and if she needs to hit something or someone.

A thin old man with a walker is near the door, arguing with Neil about something.

Even half asleep, it only takes her a moment to figure out what's being said.

"You could have hit me, didn't you think!" The old man shouts, "What's goin' on in that head of yours? If anything at all!"

Neil's trying to defend himself, "But, I mean, I thought you were one of them! A zombie!"

"Thought?" The old man sputters, "Then you should have just killed me! Not alerted every damn thing in the area!"

"I didn't! You're doing that right now!"

"And you don't think that racket would attract anything?"

Penelope thinks she understands, but she shakes her head, hoping it makes more sense.

"We can't find anything down here; how would they?"

The man grunts, "Cause they have more brain cells than you do."

"That's just mean," Neil says, shrinking in on himself.

"Just like your mother not aborting ya and saving the rest of us from your idiocy."

"What the hell is going on?" Penelope asks, swinging herself out of the bed. That was a little too far.

"This idiot threw something at me!" The old man blusters, "Made enough noise. I wouldn't be surprised if we had to deal with a swarm of those things here in a minute!"

Neil splutters and says, "I threw a knife at you. It was supposed to hit and kill you silently-"

"And look at how that turned out!"

"You tried to kill him?" Penelope asks, still a little fuzzy from sleep and confused.

"Neil, what were you thinking!" Melissa yells more than she asks.
The old man shakes his head, "That was incredibly foolish!"

"What if you had killed him?" Teagan asks, "He's just an old man."

"We don't know him!" Neil defends, "What if he's infected?"

"And that makes him less worthy to live?"

"You were just going to kill him outright!"

"I thought he was a zombie! I heard the old man coming, and with how he shuffled along, I thought it was a zombie. Can you really blame me?"

"Yes!" Teagan says, "He has a walker!"

"I am too tired for this shit; he's obviously not dead; we're not going to kill him now. I'm going to sleep, and if anyone wakes me up without the threat of zombies or food, I'm going to kill them." Penelope tells them. "I'm not joking."

"We all need to rest, and we can't if we're yelling at each other like lunatics." Teagan pacifies.

"I'll just go," the old man says, "I wasn't trying to get everything all riled up."

"Not your fault in any of this," Teagan says before asking, "Are you infected?"

"I don't know, I don't think so." The old man shuffles a little closer. "I don't even know how it's getting around."

"Have you been bit? Or get their spit in any wounds you may have?"

"No, I haven't been hurt at all."

That surprised Penelope, but maybe he'd been able to fight them off with his walker.

"Good, you can take this bunk. We'll figure out what to do later." Penelope offers, moving up to the top bunk now.

Neil scoffs, "Who died and put you in charge?"

"No clue," Penelope settles into the bed, "but enough people did that leadership has come down to me."

"Come on, I think there's better things we-" Neil starts.

Penelope cuts him off. "Shut up or get out. We need rest, we need food, and we need to get off this ship. Maybe not in that order, but resting is the only thing that won't get us killed right now."

"I'm sure you think that-" Neil starts again before getting cut off again.

"Look at them, Neil. Her arms are torn to shreds," Brody says, gesturing at Teagan, then at Courtney, "And I think she's still bleeding. Penelope's right. We've been up for hours, and we need to rest, then we can figure out where to go from here."

Penelope nods, immeasurably grateful for Brody backing her up.

Neil grumps but settles down, making it clear he's only doing it because he wants to.

"Charlie, why don't you sleep up here with me?" Penelope asks, "I don't think Teagan or Courtney will be able to get into this bunk."

"Well, if you need someone to sleep with you," Neil leers from his place on the floor.

"And that's why I asked the kid," Penelope says, moving so Charlie, who looks very grateful, can join her.

"Excuse me, sir," Brody gets the man's attention, "Why don't you take the bed, and someone else can watch in the meantime?"

"Thank you, but it's not needed, Son. I don't sleep much these days anyway, but I can still shout and holler like no one's business if needed." The old man nods at Penelope. She'll have to learn his name soon. After she sleeps.

"I'll stay up, too," Teagan says, which helps ease Penelope's anxiety." I feel bad. You didn't get to rest at all earlier."

"Alright. Sleep well, everyone. We're going to need to figure out food tomorrow."

CHAPTER 16

17

Chapter 17

In the morning, or rather, sometime the next day, they plan where to go next.

Even though it should have been a simple discussion, it went around and around. There were so many possibilities and problems that they all merged together. But eventually, now that they're not completely exhausted, they devise something like a good plan—at least they'll all agree to.

They'll head to the kitchen and pick up anything that's still safe to eat; how many days had it been down the line? It'd been four days, maybe five? Then, check the lifeboats.

From there, back to the mainland? Or trying to get southeast until they reach the mainland.

Penelope dislikes only one part of the plan: They don't know how much noise the lifeboats will make when released. They might also make a lot of noise when tossed in, which might result in many of the infected jumping in with them.

It's not ideal in the slightest, but it's also their last resort.

Getting down to where the kitchen is is easy; the kitchen itself is untouchable; there are just too many of the infected in that area, and they're making too much noise to think they could sneak past. It's not any one of them. It'd be easy if it was. Courtney just can't wait.

A brief argument is had for getting to the ships immediately, but they're all starving.

Even if they managed to get to the boats, they would probably not last long with the little food they had.

"What are we going to do then?" Neil asks the group. Well, whining to the group would be a more accurate description. "Just starve when we get to shore?"

Penelope pauses, "Aren't you from the area? Don't you know anything about surviving here?"

"Dude, just cause I'm from here doesn't mean I'm some- macho survivalist type!" Neil defends himself, not that anyone would have ever called him that.

"I thought all the kids had to do a survival trip thing?" Courtney asks.

Neil sighs. "That's just Ketchikan; they're a special kind of weirdos."

"Look, we need food before we get off of here, or I'm going to kill and eat someone," Melissa says. "Without getting infected."

Courtney, Penelope, and Teagan respond at the same time.

"Same." "Mood." "Totally."

They giggle for a second, making the men nervous.

Then Penelope remembers, "Wait, we had that canned salmon we couldn't get into; maybe other people will have stuff kept in their rooms?"

"And if it's canned? What are we going to do?" Neil whines again.

"Charlie's got a kitchen knife," Courtney says, "I can open a can with a kitchen knife."

"I think we may have mixed up the person who could survive in the wilderness." Melissa half whispers to Brody, who muffles a snort.

"Only if I have canned food and a knife," Courtney replies with as much dignity as a cat just released from where their claw was stuck.

... — — — ... ... — — — ... ... — — — ...

They head to the rooms, hoping other people stashed food, even though they almost certainly wouldn't need to for any reason other than frugality.

The starboard seemed to have fewer infected, though they couldn't find a good reason.

Theorizing could wait until they had food or knew where it was.

A few cabins are open, and the doors never shut behind them or are knocked open by someone or something. There's not much in most of them, though. Clothes, personal items, and toys are the worst.

The food is gone, nothing but scraps left.

The group spreads out; most cabins are too small for multiple people to search.

Courtney's a little feverish, though there's no sign of the black veins, and she stands at the window of one of the cabins, just looking out.

There's not much to see out there, just the dark skies and darker water, but she's not in a state to look for anything anyway. After everything, she was weaker than the others, and she'd been eating less from the start.

Why had she decided to focus on her figure? On her looks? When she was done here, she wouldn't limit anything she ate ever again.

A small noise draws her attention, and she spots an aggressive orange boat floating away.

Courtney freezes. Is that really one of the lifeboats?

She calls out when she sees the lifeboat floating away. She's not sure that's what it is, but they can't miss it. "Hey! HEY! Up here!"

Waving her arms while shouting definitely gets her friends' attention, if not the attention of the escape vessel.

"Courtney, what are you doing?" Penelope hisses, trying to quiet her.

"There's a boat! A lifeboat! Hey! Up here! We gotta get their attention!"

"You're joking!" Penelope rushes to the window, too.

"No, look, it's right there! Up here!" Immediately, they're all freaking out; this might be their best chance of.

They have to get somewhere their calls will be heard. They have to get off this ship. They hadn't been able to take a lifeboat themselves. They were just trying to survive, really.

They hang over the railing, yelling to get the tiny life vessel's attention. It's too far to swim and getting farther with two people paddling from inside.

"They're not even looking back. Do they even hear us?" Melissa asks, looking at the others for some response.

"Just yell louder!" Courtney yells. "Hey!"

They all yell hard, as loud as they can, but if the lifeboat notices, they don't turn back.

It quickly disappears behind them, presumably puttering towards land.

"They didn't stop," Melissa says, "They didn't turn back. Did they even look?

"They had to have heard us, right?" Courtney tries to ask the others, "Heard us calling for them to turn back? That there were other survivors?"

"How could they not turn back?" Penelope asks.

"No, you just didn't yell loud enough," Neil spits.

Brody turns on his friend, "Didn't yell loud enough? Where were you just now?"

"Actually yelling my head off!" Neil defends, poking Brody in the chest. "The way you should have-"

They all want to blame the others for their mistake, but Charlie's scream cuts it all off, shockingly shrill.

Several of the bodies they'd thought were dead start moving, twitching, and crawling towards them, slower than some of the ones still running around. But they're getting up and getting closer, and they're not the only ones; the other infected nearby are getting louder, smacking into things, banging against things.

Riling each other up.

The old man beats the zom- the thing at the door while the others look for other escape routes.

But all their escape routes are being cut off too fast by their yelling.

"Shit, shit, why did we do that? Shit!" Penelope says, fear in her eyes.

"We're going to die in this room," Teagan says, backing away from the door.

"I have an idea!" Brody yells, running to the balcony.

"What are you doing? We can't outswim them!" Courtney yells, pain pulsing through her at the thought.

"Hold on," Brody returns to the balcony railing and crawls up. Courtney has no idea what he's doing or if he'll succeed, but she's watching, waiting to see if he slips.

But he shocks them all by getting to the next balcony and then the one above it.

Brody disappears, and Courtney's sure that he's abandoned them all; he's going to leave them all to die.

She looks at the door Penelope and Henry are holding shut, and she knows they're going to die because Brody just left them. If she becomes one of those things, she's going to do everything in her power to find and kill him specifically.

"It's safe up here! The coast is clear! Start climbing; I'll help you up!"

Oh! He didn't abandon them!

Neil's there first, pushing Courtney out of the way. He moves surprisingly fast, and she's sure he's willing to leave them all behind, but he pauses on the next floor to start helping lift the others up to the next floor, too.

Courtney's wounds scream at her, but this is their best chance.

... — — ... ... — — — ... ... — — — ...

Penelope hadn't thought they could escape by crawling outside the ship. And yet, they are desperately climbing up and hoping the door will hold just a little longer.

The infected were battering the door. She could feel it as they held the door shut.

She was sure it was only a matter of time, though.

Courtney goes up first. Her wounds were probably the most severe, and she wouldn't be able to make it on her own. Melissa and Teagan were both raring to go and would also need help, but they would probably need less help than her.

The door shakes harder, and all left is her, Teagan, the old man, and the kid.

Nodding to Henry, Penelope rushes to help Teagan, but her wounds will make it harder for her to get up.

Penelope wishes she'd taken that firefighter course her college friend had taken. It would have been more useful, and it would have helped her here. But no, she didn't want to go to school on Saturdays.

Teagan's already crawling up to the next floor while Neil reaches to help the next person.

Penelope knows she can get up on her own. The adrenaline coursing through her body makes everything feel a bit weightless. But Charlie's too short to get up on his own, and the old man isn't strong enough.

They have to get him up next; they're not just going to leave him behind.

The old guy isn't as heavy as he looks, but lifting him without hurting him is challenging. He winces when they grab too hard, and Penelope knows he's hurting more than he's letting on. Still, between her and

Charlie helping lift him, they get the old guy onto the next floor.

The door slams open, and infected fill the room, heading right for her.

They have to keep climbing; they're out of options.

Penelope throws Charlie over her shoulder to climb, strength flooding her as the infected get close—too close. She doesn't have time for the others to help her because they're right there.

Charlie is dragged off her, but not before she feels hands grabbing her.

They're pulling, dragging, fingers gouging into her leg.

She kicks with everything she has to get them off, connecting with a sickening crunch.

Penelope drags herself onto the next floor, looking down to see the infected pushing so hard they break the railing and rain into the ocean.

18

Chapter 18

Penelope pants as she leans against the balcony railing, listening to the screeched howls of the infected two floors down. They're loud, they're way too loud. They'll need to move again, and soon.

Will the infected on other floors come to the racket they'd just left behind?

There was no telling.

That was close, way too close, way, way, way, WAY too close.

Her shoe was missing; her sock had fallen off with it. There were red gouges in her calf and ankle, but no blood. She probably hadn't been infected then. But that was so close, too close. They could have knocked her into the sea with them. She could be drowning with them.

If the others were talking, Penelope couldn't hear it over the pounding in her ears.

She's pulled away from the balcony by Brody, who sits on the bed in the room and then rubs her face and hair with a towel, concern as evident on his face as the blood staining his shirt.

It was raining?

It was Southeast Alaska. It's mostly rainforest. Of course, it was raining.

She tunes in to what the others are saying, at least trying to.

They can't keep running around the ship like this, and holing up somewhere hasn't worked this far either. Someone says that everywhere they've tried to hole up has been invaded.

It could be that because they stayed in lower areas of the shop, it made sense that they'd mostly work their way down, right?

They need help and need to make sure help is coming. The Coast Guard wouldn't leave a plague ship going. Someone should have stopped the ship by now. They shouldn't still be moving forward.

At the very least, they should be kept in a port or something, right? With doctors to figure out what's going on?

The last thing the captain said was they were still heading to Vancouver, but that couldn't be right. Most of the people on the ship were US citizens, so they should be stopping in a US port to deal with it, right?

But they hadn't said anything about that; there haven't been any announcements since. How long has it been?

Penelope couldn't remember or even remember the last time she'd eaten.

Help was probably coming, though, right?

It had to.

But they don't know if help is coming, and it probably isn't if no one's on the bridge. They don't even know if help was called for.

They know the rough timeline; Penelope had read the notes, but that was days ago, and the first known infection was well over a week ago. They had to have called the Coast Guard before that, right?

They don't know that for sure, though. They know the ship hasn't changed directions in days, and it's been six or more days since they'd been told to stay in their rooms.

And even if she thought they weren't being guided to Vancouver, they were still going in the right direction; where were they supposed to make port? Were they even headed toward land? They could be headed toward the middle of the Pacific. They'd have no way of knowing if they'd been turned at night.

It'd been a long time since she could remember seeing land, and they didn't even know the lifeboat's direction. They'd assumed it was going toward land, but they didn't know for sure; it'd left their sight so fast.

They need to get off this ship, food, rest, and weapons.

Any of these would be hard enough on its own, but it's all of them that's causing them to struggle.

They're already down so many weapons, too.

Charlie's had been lost by Neil, and Penelope had dropped hers and her phone while moving between the balconies. They didn't have Courtney's weapons either. Teagan had an IV pole she'd snagged earlier, but it wasn't good in close quarters, and it wasn't like she could use it well in her current state.

Getting weapons was a good idea first. Keep the others off them while they search, but they're all getting weak from hunger, too. They hadn't found much earlier, and anything they'd found was lost, swarmed by the infected.

They need rest. They need food. They need off the ship.

How did they get off the ship?

They could try to find where the brig was; there's a chance they'd find weapons there.

But they wouldn't find food or anything down there.

They could look at the kitchen again, but it was trashed the last time they went, and there were so many infected when they left.

It wasn't safe, especially not without real weapons.

Neil suggests going down into the ship's depths and turning off the engine so they don't crash into the shore; he thinks it'll give them more time to plan an actual plan when Penelope cuts him off.

She suggests heading to the uppermost deck—the infected probably won't be up there—they might be able to see some of what's going on or where they are.

Neil's pissy she interrupted his idea—or because it could save them—possibly give them time to figure something out.

Penelope argues that it'll be safer. They'll be able to figure out where they are—something they don't know right now—and they'll be able to contact the Coast Guard. They might even have food or weapons up there.

The others like her idea more than going to the engine room. Neil's salty about it but finally agrees.

She's pretty smart, after all.

...— — —... ...— — —... ...— — —...

They rest in the room for a little while, catching their breaths, but the room is too small for all of them to stay. It would probably be uncomfortable if the group were even half the size.

Add to that Neil is still too interested in her—way too curious, uncomfortably interested—and you have a recipe for Penelope figuratively climbing the walls.

Penelope would literally rather be stuck in this situation with a grizzly. She wanted to be anywhere, literally, anywhere else, then trapped with Neil asking way too many borderline personal questions. Not just borderline; they were way too personal, but he didn't seem to catch or care if she was uncomfortable being asked.

They've left the rooms, creeping along quietly.

Well, as quietly as the rest of them could because Neil couldn't, wouldn't shut up.

Penelope wishes she had something sharp enough to cut out his tongue, but sadly, they're all out.

This forced her to keep responding to Neil. If she didn't answer, he would ask the question again, louder, because he hadn't gotten the hint that it was not the time. This is the worst time to ask questions, let alone ones like these. If he's not careful, he'll bring more infected on them.

But he still asks, and she has to answer because even though she's doing the minimum to respond, even though the others have shushed him for asking louder questions when she didn't respond enough for his apparent liking, he gets louder.

They're going to have to kill him or leave him behind because he really is going to get them killed.

He was.

Because he wanted to know her goddamn bra size and then wanted to tell self-aggrandizing stories about how he could tell most women's bra size at a glance.

But they don't run into any of the infected in some reverse miracle. So she can't just throw him to the infected and pretend it was an accident.

When they get to the topmost floor, they look around, looking for anyone, anything.

"Spread out. There might be another first aid kit or something else we can use up here," Penelope says, helping Courtney sit.

Neil continues to hover too close, "Do you really think we'll find anything up here?"

She doesn't want to respond, but luckily, Courtney does: "We might. You never know. I mean, there's like nothing up here, but who knows?"

"Neil, can you keep an eye on Courtney for me? Kay, thanks, bye." Penelope leaves the two of them before either can complain.

She carries her weapon carefully, looking for anything useful. She's now too vigilant of the possibility of zom- of infection- behind any door.

"Oh god!" Melissa half shouts, pulling everyone's attention to a hidden-away corner barely covered by an overhang.

"What is it?" Penelope asks, but Melissa's already pointing.

A body, someone obviously dead, hypothermia, Penelope would think, given he doesn't have any obvious wounds and that he's nearly naked. Teagan had told her that when she'd learned about it, paradoxical undressing. When people were so cold, they thought they were hot and took off their clothes.

When had it happened? His skin was bloated and waterlogged, and his lips blue. This man has been dead for a while, days even.

Had he been up here, slowly freezing to death, while Penelope, Courtney, and Teagan were still in their room, complaining about the internet?

"Oh." Penelope manages to choke out, shocked to be at the mercy of a whirlwind of emotions. This man hadn't died from an attack but from the elements, something that shouldn't happen on a cruise of all places. "Well, come on. No use in gawking."

It's harder than she thought to pull her gaze away from the dead man.

They have to keep looking and see if they could use anything.

Teagan checks the body, too, just to make sure, but it's evident from looking at him he'd been dead a while. She confirms what Penelope had thought; he'd frozen to death, and the rain and wind got him.

All the lifeboats are gone at this point. The one they'd seen float off was probably the last, and it's long since floated into the distance.

"Alright, so there's no one up here. Surprisingly, no one is infected, and no one else is still alive." Once they've all reassembled, Penelope tells the rest, "It's still raining, and we're going to end up like our buddy over there if we're not careful."

"Well. There's not much we can use as weapons up here safely, but maybe if we lower our standards to look around again?" Brody asks.

"Might be for the best; there's just not enough weapons between us," Penelope says, and they all quietly ignore the fact that, at the very least, Teagan and Courtney are going to be at a disadvantage no matter what, and the old man, Henry, she'd finally learned was his name probably wasn't going to be able to protect himself without his walker. "Really, anything would work at this point."

Penelope looks around the edges again, seeing the lack of lifeboats again. She wants to rage about it, wants to be furious, wants to be able to wish pain and hardships on all of the people who left them all here.

But she can't.

Even though it would be easy to want the worst for them, she just hopes those people make it to shore safely, that they'll be okay, and that she and her friends will be okay.

She can't fault them for trying to survive, just like her and her friends. If they'd found the lifeboat and been the ones floating off, she's not sure she'd turn around and get that close to the ship again.

The way the infected had flooded off the balcony.

Penelope shivers; now that she's seen that, she knows they couldn't have turned back.

Another thing they can see from up top is that they're all over the place. They can see the ones hanging over the railings, the ones that seem to just be doing laps of the covered parts of the ship, and some of the ones that are simply lying somewhere, but Penelope is sure they're just waiting for a chance, something to come to life and kill someone.

It's just so much, too much.

They're just so many of them.

A ship of thousands never feels as full as it does when it's full of the infected. The undead.

Only half noticing as others join her for her slow walk around the end of the deck as she looks down at the horror of the disease that's spread over the ship.

She's not the only one who doesn't know what to do as they look around, horror growing at the destruction of the ship. How would they even get off? There was only ocean for miles in every direction.

They couldn't even see the coastline anymore.

But she didn't think there was anything out there, anywhere in visible distance. The drizzle was turning into a heavy rain, and they didn't have cover out here.

How far away from land are they now?

How will they get off the ship? If they dove in and swam, would they be followed in?

Were they really all alone here, with no help coming from anywhere? Were they too far away from land to get a signal to the Coast Guard?

Someone surely had to have called for help. They had to. All this happened, and someone had to call for help. But if help isn't coming, how long do they have? How much longer until the little food they have runs out?

Would it be better to run into shore?

It would be easier to get off the ship, but would it be? Would they get hurt if they crashed? Were they sure they were even heading to shore?

She looks for any sign of living people anywhere on the ship, and that's when Penelope spots the bridge. It's a couple floors down from them. They just need to get in to see if they can make it easier for themselves, maybe even keep the crash from killing them—if they're even heading toward shore.

"Come on, we might be able to just climb down to it instead of going back down the stairs and around to it," Penelope says, looking for any obvious route down the road.

The others look down, then at her.

"What is it?" Charlie asks.

"The bridge. That's where they control the whole ship from." Penelope leans over the railing a bit, trying to spot a ladder or something. "It's right there; if we can get into it from the outside, we might be able to at least figure out where we're going."

"How are we even supposed to get in, though?" Teagan says,

following Penelope.

"Okay, we might not be able to normally, but if we break one of the windows to get in, we'll have an easy entrance." Penelope's sure there's a ladder, something. They've have to crawl around on the outside of that room somehow, which means there's gotta be a way to it.

Henry hems. "I'm not sure you'll be able to break the glass, though. It is supposed to be able to withstand things crashing into it. Waves, fish, whatnot."

"The stuff down low is, but the glass up here isn't that strong or even reinforced. They have completely different problems if the water splashes up here." Penelope says, spotting a ladder without any safety features. "There. That's how we'll get down."

"Then I guess I have nothing else to say but good luck, sweetheart. I'll be waiting for ya."

Penelope feels her heart grow at Henry's smile. Even though buckets of rain are pouring down, she's sure he will stand guard as long as it takes for her to try to get in and give the rest of them the go-ahead.

19

Chapter 19

Slip sliding down to the room is somehow the most terrifying thing she's done so far.

Even counting finding out there were infected and being chased by them.

The rainwater turned everything into a waterslide, frictionless and cold, and if it wasn't for Brody and Neil helping her down, Penelope's sure she would have just kept slipping until she fell off the ship. Ladder be damned.

Penelope lays on the cold, wet, slippery metal that makes up the ship and feels the cold, heavy rain pounding on her. With a deep breath, she slowly scoots forward until she's hanging over the top of the deck and can peek in the windows.

Inside, the room is full of obviously infected people. There's more than Penelope had expected, a few wandering around listlessly looking thin and starved, as well as a couple dead ones on the ground. They might have also been dead humans. It was hard to be sure.

Up close like this, they can see the small walkway going all the way around the cabin and the doors leading out to it. They can use those to get in. They'll be able to leave the door to the rest of the ship locked and keep themselves safe from anything on the rest of the ship. The main door looks sturdy, too; it would probably be safer there than just about anywhere else.

Plus, there are extra routes out of the room, just in case.

Quietly, Penelope tells the others that she thinks it would be best to try to lure out the ones they can and then deal with the rest. It's nearly impossible to tell the corpse-like infected from the bodies on the ground, and any might pop up to bite them.

Brody nods, dark hair slowly matting to his head under the force of the rain. "I like it; definitely less dangerous. But how are we going to deal with them without putting ourselves in danger? There's really not enough room for us to move around without risking falling overboard with the infected if they go down."

Penelope pauses, thinking, "Maybe we stay up here and just open the door and make noise?"

"Like-" Brody gestures in a way too big motion, nearly hitting Neil, whose thin overshirt isn't doing much against the rain, but it's probably doing more than Penelope's tank top. "Draw them over and leave them on the walkway?"

"I'm thinking they might push each other off the boat," Penelope says with a small shoving motion, "like they did earlier."

"There's not that many of them this time, though, I don't know if they'll break the railing this time."

"They might still knock each other over," Penelope says.

"Good point." Brody nods, "What do we do if they don't fall over?"

With a shrug, Penelope offers, "Push them over?"

"It's risky, but it might work."

"At worst, maybe we can distract them while someone sneaks in and pushes them over the edge?" Penelope offers.

Brody shakes his head, "I don't like that; it puts one person in too much danger."

"We kinda always in danger right now, and it'll keep-"

"LEROY JENKINS!"

Penelope's head spins as Neil shouts and drops to the little balcony; Brody tries to stop him and falls right behind him, landing much harder as he couldn't brace himself for the fall. Neil's already shouting and rattling the door like there's no tomorrow, and the infected all rush toward him and toward the door.

"Brody!" Penelope throws herself down. The only thought in her mind is protecting Brody where he's fallen and maybe pushing some of the infected overboard. Penelope's unprepared for the sheer numbers, for how they push, shove, and grab at anything and everything.

She's pushed against the railing, one snapping and scratching at her.

With a blow stronger than she'd thought she could manage, she knocks that one off herself, taking the opportunity to look for the others.

Neil's gotten into the room and looks massively overwhelmed by the infected, blood already covering him from where they're scratching the hell out of him. Brody is up, at least, pushing in and trying to keep them away from her.

God, this all went so wrong so fast; how could Neil have been so stupid?

She can't just stand here; she's got to do something; the others aren't going to come down and help.

Penelope makes a choice, and she's aware of how stupid a choice it is even as she makes it, but she's gotta try to kill the infected, or at least distract them. They need this room, they're not going to survive if they can't get in here, and if they fail now, they're not going to survive anyway.

Somehow, somewhen, she's going to figure out how to make that noise again, on purpose. Now, though, the horrifying, scared, angry undulation that comes out of her throat when she tries to get the infected's attention is unintentional.

The noise stops everyone and everything in the room for a moment, and then they all move toward her, which is not the plan.

Too late now, though.

She rushes back toward the other door, pushing it open, and tries to lead the infected outside, hoping it will work.

And it does mostly; many infected tumble over the railing trying to get to her, but not all of them.

Penelope gets knocked onto the walkway, one of the infected right on her. Fighting back is out of the question, with it lying on her. The chair leg in her hands is the only thing standing between her and the zombie. She can't move, can't roll out of the way, and doesn't have the strength to push it off.

It's gnashing its teeth, half words dripping from its mouth with copious drool; Penelope feels the room-temperature spit land on her face and chest. She tries to keep her mouth shut; she doesn't know if it'll spread if it gets into her eyes. All she can do is keep it from biting her, screaming again, the undulating trill again, and wondering absently if that's how she screams now.

Then, like an angel from above, Teagan appears, using the IV pole to spear the one on Penelope, not getting it off her but pulling it back so she can scramble back, get up, and attempt to bash its brains in.

She looks at Teagan, both panting.

Part of her wonders how Teagan got down here and what she was thinking rushing in like that, but she's also very, very glad that she had. She's also very, very thankful and wants to hug her friend.

Looking into the room, the group managed to kill off the infected. Maybe her plan had worked in spite of Neil. Courtney and Melissa had come down, too, and looked like they'd more than done their own parts. Both were bleeding through their bandages again and looked on the verge of passing out. But they were alive and didn't look more injured than they had been.

Penelope wipes the spit off her face over and over, trying to get the phantom touch of it off of her, trying to forget how it'd felt to have it drip onto her, viscus and slimy and ugh!

Penelope was fine physically but terrified emotionally and mentally. She was also pretty sure she was in shock again; still might be a better way of putting it.

She rubs a hand over her face again. She didn't think there were any wounds on her face, anywhere the virus could creep in, but it was too close, much too close.

She could have died if Teagan wasn't there; she would have died.

She might die anyway.

20

NOT DONE

The first thing they try is the steering wheel, but because things can never be easy for them, it's essentially locked in place. They can't spin it, and there are no indicators when they apply any pressure to it.

So, as far as options go, they are obviously out; they need to find another way of dealing with this and figure something out.

They look over the whole terminal-looking thing, but there are so many buttons, screens, and more. How are they supposed to figure it out? And many of them are covered in more information than they know how to interpret.

They all look at everything, but it's locked, turned off, or disconnected. Some of the screens and panels have been smashed.

Penelope wonders if that was done before or after the virus set in, if it was done to help, or if it was done for a reason. If something had blinked the wrong way, and now what they needed was gone, they'd be stuck here until it crashed or they died.

Even though she's the tech person who might be able to figure this out, she doesn't want to slow down, stop, or think.

Instead, she gets back out into the pouring rain.

Penelope climbs back up to Charlie and Henry and tries to figure out how to get them both down without hurting anyone.

They find some stuff they can use as rope and climb down, but it's a slow process, with too many stops for Henry. He's an old man, but the slow climb wracks her nerves. She's sure something will pop up while she holds the rope and keeps them from slipping.

Eventually, they're all down in the bloody bridge. Penelope settles Henry into the captain's chair; it's the only one that looks comfortable and the least they can do for him. The step up almost does him in; he's obviously exhausted, and Penelope wonders if it would have been better to just slide him down rather than let him climb.

He's safe for now, at least, and she'll count it as a win if he doesn't have a heart attack soon.

There's more to do, so much more, but taking care of their people is more important. Penelope checks on Teagan's wounds. They're inflamed and probably infected, but not with the mystery disease. She's feverish and radiating heat, but there's not much they can do about that. There hadn't been any antibiotics they could easily take from the infirmary, and she was probably well beyond what antibiotic pills could do for her now.

Henry looks at everything while the rest get rid of the bodies.

"You know," Henry starts, almost conversationally, "I've got at least a little experience on different vessels from my time in the service."

Penelope nods, checking on Courtney. Her wounds are in better shape than Teagan's, probably because they were able to clean and bandage hers immediately.

"And although this is very different from the vessels I've been on before, I'm sure we're on a course for land."

Penelope gives him her full attention, "You're sure about this?"

"Yep. We'll get there eventually, though we're aimed a lot further down the coast than our original heading."

"Do you know where we're going? How long it'll be?"

"Well, if we don't take too much damage or something else terrible doesn't happen to the ship in the meantime, we'll probably make land somewhere in Oregon, possibly California." Henry taps on one of the screens. "I can't tell you how long it'll be, though. It'll depend on our speed and our exact heading."

"Can you guess?"

"Maybe a few days? A little longer if the currents are against us, less if they're with us."

Penelope doesn't know how he knows, but she's thankful he does. At least it can give them something like a timeline.

"Okay, we can work with that. Can you stop it or turn it around? Something?"

"I'm sorry, Penelope." Henry shakes his head, "I don't know how they've got some kind of code or lock or something on it."

"That's okay, Henry. At least we know what's going on, where we're going." She weakly smiles, "It's better than the pure unknown before, even if it worsens our timeline."

Penelope focuses on checking on Courtney but looks around to see the others taking this their first real chance to relax.

She's about to do the same when she looks at Neil and nearly explodes into a fiery rage. What was he thinking? Had he really thought that was a good idea? He could have gotten them killed! They all could have been killed.

Penelope couldn't find it in herself to care what he was thinking; she just wanted to slap him or throw him overboard so she didn't have to look at his dumb face that was looking more and more like a good target.

They'd been coming up with a plan, a good one! And he went and not only put all of their lives in danger but almost got her killed.

She wipes her face again, just to be sure, just to be safe.

It was so close, too close, way, way too close.

No. Courtney needs her attention, and they need to rest. Afterward, she could look around and see if there was anything else she could do to help them.

Rewrapping Courtney's wounds uses up the last of their gauze. They'd need more soon. They didn't have a way to clean the stuff they had, and their chance of infection was too high if they left it on.

Penelope looks around for any signs of what happened. If there's any information about what happened up here. Suppose she doesn't have something to focus on or something to do. In that case, Penelope's going to tear Neil to shreds figuratively, then literally, and then feed him to the infected.

Since she doesn't know anything about boats, ships, or cruise ships, she doesn't even bother looking for anything that might be able to stop the ship. It's a lost cause, and even if she did know how to stop it, what would they do then? Just float on a ship in the middle of the ocean with a bunch of the zombi- infected people? Instead, she looks for anything about the infection and the actions they might have taken.

They might be able to give anything to someone, the CDC, their rescuers, someone.

It probably won't help them to know what happened, but she wants to get her mind off of it all, to not think about how close to death she'd been.

She still felt too close to it now.

And she'd lost her phone.

She's trying to get some of the consoles to work, but they're locked or frozen onto whatever information they're showing. She's assuming that's the right thing for most of them; you wouldn't want information switching around willy-nilly, but how was she supposed to find anything that had been going on?

Neil slides up beside her, all faux suave and smooth, "Hey there. I noticed you're messing around with the computers. You know, I'm something of an IT guy myself. Never had an official job doing it, but

I'm the guy everyone calls when they can't get their computer working."

But Penelope completely ignores him and won't even look at him. Knows deep within her that if she looks at him, acknowledges him at all, she'll turn into a screaming banshee and might literally tear his head off with her bare hands.

"It's okay if you don't want to ask for help; figuring out some machines is a big task."

She won't look at him, can't. She nearly died because of this idiot.

"It might be easier to focus on-" He's starting again, and Penelope is just going to kill him; she is. He's basically asking for it.

Henry notices her rage or his idiocy and says, "Excuse me, young man. Neil, was it?"

Neil pauses, "Yeah?"

"I think you would be more help with removing the bodies from the room. Penelope here seems to know what she's doing as far as the machines here."

"Well, I mean, it really looks like the others have it covered."

"And Penelope has the computers covered. Go help with the bodies. They definitely need help. And I'm sure Penelope will ask for help if she needs it." Henry's voice leaves no room for question, and she silently cheers for him saying something.

After all, these bodies might have been outside, or at least not in the room, if he'd only listened to them.

If he'd only waited instead of jumping in like an idiot.

He could help clean up the mess.

There was a lot of mess on the floor, blood, and more body parts than she wanted to think about—How many people had been in here?—and lots of papers scattered around, though they don't have anything she understands.

She thanks Henry when Neil's outside, though the man only smiles in response.

Eventually, hidden underneath other stuff, she finds a tablet that still turns on.

Unfortunately, it's locked.

She shouldn't bother with it, shouldn't try guessing, should just move on to the next thing, but she wants to try to guess the passcode, just to see if she can.

And wouldn't you know it, it's all zeros.

It still has the information of whoever last pulled it up, and it's a lot of information.

It contains everything she was looking for in the form of a series of incident logs. There's some stuff on it that she already knew about, such as the infected man and his wife. But they knew about the infected individual and the attacks early on. He'd been a problem long before ending up in the infirmary.

It's not too surprising. The medical center had had that, but at least they'd informed the rest of the ship.

She reads them over anyway. Reads that they'd locked him up until they could get him off the ship, which wasn't included in the other files. Maybe it was a psychotic break, someone not handling things well.

They'd kept going because, well, what else would they do?

But then the victims started attacking. The captain had figured it was some kind of outbreak or possibly even someone tampering with the food supply. They'd pulled the fire doors and locked everyone in their cabins. Done everything in their power to quarantine people, but it hadn't worked.

They contacted the local authorities and then the Coast Guard, which advised them to stay in open water and quarantine everyone.

But despite the continued calls, it took nearly a day to hear back. They'd contacted the Coast Guard, who said they weren't the only ones reporting unusual activity with a potentially viral component. They were going to contact the CDC and then contact them again.

They'd heard scuttlebutt from other ships trying to contact anyone, but there didn't seem to be much help.

The crew reached out to the Coast Guard but never heard back.

21

Chapter 21

The sky darkens on day six now? Since they'd all been told to stay in their rooms. Too damn long, and it'd been too damn long since they ate, their food long since run out, and it hadn't really been enough anyway.

At this point, the only good thing about this ship was that there was running water nearly everywhere, except, of course, the control room.

She'd read somewhere that survival was about the rule of three, three minutes without oxygen, three days without water, and three weeks without food.

She was pretty sure that even if you could survive that long without food, you wouldn't be in good shape at the end. And she already felt weak, saw how weak everyone looked. They wouldn't make it that long. Teagan and Courtney definitely wouldn't; both were already injured and wasting their energy just trying to heal.

They were safe, for now. They knew where they were and where they were going but didn't know when or if help was coming.

It'd been two days since the ship last tried to contact the Coast Guard, and while they were safer up here, the control crew had still been infected. The other infected hadn't tried to come up or if they had, they went right back down. But these people had been infected somehow.

So it wasn't the perfect safe haven they'd hoped it would be, or someone could be infected without other symptoms.

"So what do we do?" Penelope asks after the bodies are gone, and they've all found somewhat clean places.

"What do you mean?" Neil asks, and rage bubbles through Penelope just seeing him. But she doesn't have the energy for it.

"We need to get off the ship. If we can't direct it, can't stop it, we're going to need help." She says instead of calling him an idiot like she's like to.

"What are you thinking?" Brody asks, pulling Melissa closer to him.

"We should try the Coast Guard; the radio should still be tuned to the right channel." She pauses. "All the last logs say that they'd already reached out to the Coast Guard, so the radio has to already be tuned to that channel."

"Do you think they'll help?" Teagan asks from her one of the officer chairs. She looks significantly less comfortable, but it's better than sitting on the floor.

"We can just call out, I think," Courtney says.

"Call out and wait for a response. If they don't respond in five minutes, call out again. Do it three times, then wait an hour to try again," Henry tells them.

"That seems like a lot of counting," Neil says, a displeased scrunch on his face.

"It's the proper procedure, boy. It keeps the airways from cluttering and ensures time for a response." Henry says, "It'll increase the chances someone hears us, and we hear them too."

"So we should just stick to whatever channel the radio is already on?"

"Start with 16," Henry says. "I think that's the emergency channel, but we should also try other channels. There's no telling who's out there listening."

"So, uh, how does it work?" Brody asks.

Luckily, the radio works like the ones on the ship the old man was on. He shows them how to use it, the procedure for calling out, and the different channels to try calling on.

While Henry shows them how to use the radio, Charlie and Penelope barricade the doors to the ship. They'll leave when it's safer to get to other parts of the ship. Or when they get a hold of someone who can help them.

They take turns calling out to the void, and Penelope hopes they reach anyone.

22

Chapter 22

Stomach rumbling, Penelope groans.

She knows they need to get food, and even though their other attempts have failed, they've got to try again.

"Alright." She claps her hands together. "How are we gonna do this?"

"Do what?" Melissa asks from where she and Brody had curled up.

"Get food. We need it. I don't know how long I can go right now." Penelope says, knowing she's not the only one

Neil's back on his shit, offering, "Well, I could try to sneak down-"

"Like that'll work." Charlie scoffs.

"But I can. One person will get down there a lot faster than multiple people!" Neil defends.

"And I'm the pope. You can't shut up long enough to get down there, get food, and get back." Penelope says, shaking her head. "It's just not possible."

"I can, too! It's not that hard." Neil blusters, an angry flush covering his face.

"For the rest of us, maybe," Penelope's hunger shoots through her, "But we're also capable of shutting our mouths for over a minute. Which I've never seen you actually do."

"Well, it's not like most of you can go anyway; look at all of you!"

Penelope does and sees her people injured, exhausted, and hungry. She feels how the rage and hunger under her own skin and wants nothing more than to rip into Neil and pull him apart.

She knows it wouldn't make her better than the infected, that even though her rage is founded, there's no place for it. She's still furious. She hates him; she hates all of this and would tear his heart out and eat it for all to see.

But that's not who she is; it's not. She's not this person.

"Well, we can't send you down alone," Penelope says, then mutters, mostly to herself. "If only to ensure the food gets back up to us."

"We need a route," Teagan says.

"We could try the kitchens?"

"You've been down there; you know there's no food there." Penelope shakes her head, "And if there was the last time we went down there. I don't think it's there anymore."

"I think our standards are low enough now for whatever was left down there," Brody says.

Melissa shakes her head, "But there were so many of them in the kitchen and the dining room. There's no way we'll be able to get past them."

"I think they've moved," Neil says, coming out of his pout, "I mean, the kitchen has to be empty with all the infected we've seen."

"That might only be a fraction of them, though." Brody cautions. "We have to be careful about it. We're literally planning to come back weighed down with food."

"It's weird more haven't gone over the edges," Penelope says, thinking about all the infected they've seen.

"What?" Neil blurts.

"The infected," Penelope says again, "As soon as it started raining hard again, they all disappeared. The outer portions of the ship are empty right now. And they're mostly inside."

"I hate to break it to ya, but most of the ship is inside," Neil says.

"No, I mean. There aren't any outside, like up on top, for example; you'd have to have a few up here, just by the nature of semi-exploring."

"Maybe they just don't like going upstairs?"

"That's possible, but we almost never see them out by the railings either. The only time they've been outside when we've been out there was before we came here. There's evidence of them, but they're never out there unless something draws them. And they disappear so fast, too."

"Maybe we're just lucky." Courtney offers, but it's hard to believe her when she's all bandaged with gauze and scabbed-over scratches.

"Or maybe it's going to be the thing that helps us; if we stay toward the outer edges of the ship, we'll be able to avoid the worst of them. We just gotta be fast about." Penelope says, looking for support.

They think before Neil asks, "So, who's going down?"

"Teagan and Courtney are out," Penelope says, then adds. "Charlie and Henry, too."

"But I can do it!" Charlie jumps up.

"Charlie, I'm not doing it to keep you out; you're the only able-bodied one of them right now."

"Wait, I'm going?" Neil asks, looking around.

Penelope lets the venom drip from her voice. "You were so eager to prove yourself earlier; it shouldn't be an issue. Right?"

Neil stutters for a moment, but nothing sensible makes it out of his mouth.

Brody talks over him, "It's going to be dangerous; there's no ifs or buts about it, and while most of us would prefer to not leave, only a few of us are still physically able to leave, including you, Neil. So, it'll be you, me, Melissa, and Penelope, and we'll get food and get back up here as soon as possible."

"Yeah, that's for the best. Do we know how long it'll take to do all this?" Melissa asks.

"No, we're just going to do it and hope we're fast."

Teagan or Courtney would be good to have with them if they weren't injured or even less injured. They need to monitor Teagan's infection. It doesn't seem like she's infected; there are no black lines. But it's another thing to worry about.

Anything left in the infirmary is probably ruined. The infected were right behind them when they abandoned it, but there's no way to be sure without checking.

Penelope would prefer to leave Neil behind, but they need him to carry things. Charlie would probably be just as good, but he's already been in the line of fire too much, and she wants to keep him out of it if they can avoid it. Unfortunately, Neil can probably carry more than she can; she can still protect them if they find food. Though she'd prefer they not run into anything or anyone.

23

Chapter 23

There's a little more discussion. They share thoughts on what else they could grab while out and about, what else they'd need. But it would be too dangerous to go anywhere without a plan, and even now, though they have a plan, it's not the best one they could have.

They each have a weapon or something they can use as a weapon.

And leave the others with the one remaining. Well, leave Charlie with the remaining weapon, as he's the only one who can defend himself properly if something happens. Courtney and Henry might, with emphasis on might, be able to protect themselves. But Teagan's getting weaker and less grounded as time passes, and Penelope's getting more worried.

Finally, Penelope, Neil, Brody, and Melissa are as ready as they'll ever be.

Charlie closes the door behind them.

Fortunately, there aren't any zom—any infected.

Penelope says, "Alright, I want to go over the plan one more time, just to be safe-"

"No." Melissa snaps at her, "It's a waste of time. We *know* what we're doing; we *know* we'll get food. End of story."

But Penelope shakes her head, "I just want to make sure we all know the plan. I want us, all of us, to get out of this alive, and that's easier if we know what we're going to do."

"Pen, if we repeat the plan one more time, I'll know it by rote," Melissa says.

"It's okay, Penelope. We know what the plan is." Brody reassures her.

But the grumbled twisting of her stomach makes her worry nonetheless. Hunger and nerves shot anxiety through her.

They all creep down, preparing for a fight but hoping to sneak past anything they might meet. Any corner might have an infected, and anywhere might have another survivor who won't think twice before swinging.

Penelope is worried they'll get lost and wants to be sure of what they'll do if, no, when, they get there and need to get back.

The halls seem longer; they've traversed the ship before, but it never took so long. They're careful, looking for any sign of infected.

It's a slow, agonizing trek, staying so quiet.

Managing to avoid making more than a whisper of sound on the carpet.

Somehow, Brody manages to make Neil shut up for the whole trek. Penelope hadn't thought it possible.

Nothing.

Around each corner.

Nothing.

The trip down is silent.

Still.

No infected on the way down.

No people.

No bodies.

Nothing.

They look for any sign of something waiting around a dark corner.

But it's only them creeping further and further.

Finally, they reach the kitchen, where there's nothing.

Well, there are still a couple of bodies, but even those aren't going to get up again.

And the one that had attacked Teagan lay where they left it. Head bashed in, covered in blood and viscera. Hands blacked with Teagan's blood, too.

Bloated, rotting thing.

Looking around with lowered standards, there's more food left than Penelope had thought. Canned foods are hopefully still safe to eat, but they still need to crack them open. A can opener and a couple more knives are tucked into their bags, too.

As they search for more food, Penelope looks for anything unusual, such as signs of other living people, signs of the infected, and signs that something or someone is about to attack.

But there's no sign of anything.

No people, no infected, nothing.

Just silence.

Not even the knocking of the engine.

She wondered if that had drawn them away. But where were they now?

They didn't know anything about the infected or how they worked. They knew sound drew them, and, if so, would that sound be loud enough to actually draw them?

It didn't matter now; getting back to the bridge mattered.

They creep back to the bridge, still careful, so very, very careful, but faster, nearly flying through the halls compared to their earlier pace.

The halls are still empty, and they might never be able to travel through the ship this easily again.

They can drop off the food and look for other things after eating.

Penelope can feel herself practically skipping at their good fortune. If they're smart about it, they might even be able to get to the infirmary and find something for Teagan's infection.

Quiet raps against the door, shave and a haircut, and the door opens.

"You'll never believe it!" Courtney says, squealing.

"What?" Penelope asks, unloading the food to a reasonably clean section.

"We got a hold of another ship!" Courtney squeals again, this time getting shushed by the others.

"Not just another ship," Henry says, looking more alive than he has, "but someone who claimed they might be able to help!"

"What?" Neil says at the same time Brody says, "That's fantastic!"

"We're getting help? When? Who?" Penelope asks, food forgotten in her excitement.

"Now, calm down, Penelope." With a good-natured smile, Henry says, "There's more you need to know."

"Like what?" Penelope does her best to reign in her excitement.

"They're a couple days out and don't know if they'll be able to intercept-" Henry's smile disappears, "but they'll try. This ship is going pretty fast, and they're a fair distance away; it'll be hard for them to get close and harder for us to get onto their smaller ship."

"But there's still a chance? They're still coming?" Penelope is ecstatic. This couldn't have come at a better time. Well, it could have, but she wants to go home. She misses her mom and her bed and not having to fight for her life.

"A few days. It's not the Coast Guard; the ship they think can get to us and match speed is further away. It needs to finish its current and get refueled first."

"I'll take it." Penelope smiles; she must be emoting too much.

But it's hope, plain and simple.

Now they have food, a ship on the way, and the infected have disappeared.

It really is the best day.

24

Chapter 24

"Be careful now, kids. You're going to want to eat a lot, and that's the worst thing you can do to yourself at this point." Henry warns them, "I know you're hungry, so am I. But we have to be careful."

"He's right." Teagan says fuzzily, "You can make yourself really sick if you overeat."

"So what should we do?" Neil asks, managing to not sound as irritating as usual.

"Maybe measure out the food before eating?" Teagan tells them, but she sounds unsure. "Really small amounts, like a mouthful or two, and then wait before eating any more."

"Right," Penelope says. Even though she correctly warned them away from eating too much, especially after they'd gone without for so long, it's hard for Penelope not to stuff herself full.

Teagan knew that the effects would be bad, and she trusts Teagan's judgment, even as obviously sick and weak as she is now.

They start by opening one of the small cans and scooping a bit. It's not much, but they need to start slow, and well, this was a slow way of doing it. It's not as much food, but they were starting small.

She doesn't complain.

"We need to make another plan. That much is clear." Penelope tells them instead of staring longingly at the small pile of food.

"For what?" Charlie asks, scraping his finger around the inside of the can, trying to get the little residue left.

"Now. If a ship is on the way, even if they're a few days out, we'll need to discuss how we're going to get onto the other ship and what we're willing to do to get there."

She doesn't add that she'd rather not be stuck on a ship with Neil any longer because he was getting on her nerves by touching all the food they had. Repeatedly.

And with food in her system, planning suddenly seems much easier.

"So what do our would-be rescuers know?"

"Not much. Our location?" Courtney says.

"We told them our current dead reckoning, speed, and what information we had from the data here, ship class, and the like." Henry corrects her.

"Anything else?"

"Well..." Courtney says, "We weren't sure what was relevant. They didn't need much more than our location and size."

"Like, how many people should they be expecting?" Penelope cracks open another can, taking her share before passing it around.

"We didn't actually tell the incoming ship how many people were on this one," Courtney admits.

Penelope looks at her. "It is a cruise, so assumably, there's a lot."

"But we're the only ones alive," Charlie says. Penelope snags the can away, realizing he's about to start licking inside the can.

Charlie pouts, but Teagan adds her own thoughts. "There's no way we're actually the only ones. They should know about that."

"We might be the only ones they'll be able to recognize as human."

"We shouldn't talk like that. Just cause we haven't bumped into people doesn't mean there aren't others." Teagan presses, "They could still be alive, just hiding somewhere, waiting on a timeline that they were given. But it's so much shorter than how long we'll probably be at sea, even without help."

"There's not much we can do to help them now. It's really a waiting game."

"No," Teagan says, sounding firmer than she had all day. "If there are still people on board, they needed to know that the ship is going to crash when it lands and that they should be at the back of the ship so they don't just die instantly."

"You're right. We do need to do something." Penelope soothes.

"Maybe we can reach out to them?" Brody asks.

"How?"

"The overhead," Brody suggests, "that'll probably be the best bet."

"But how's that going to affect everything?" Penelope asks, visions of the zombies going nuts in her head, scrabbling at the walls to find the source.

Melissa looks at her, "What do you mean?"

"We have no idea how going on the loudspeaker will affect everything. Or if there's even people." Penelope tells them, "It might doom anyone who's not somewhere safe."

"I mean, is it really something to worry about though? We haven't run into anyone." Courtney comments.

"Courtney, Melissa, Brody, and Neil weren't with us when this started. We bumped into them." Penelope tells her.

"And you literally ran into Charlie," Teagan adds.

"We picked up Henry along the way the way too. He wasn't there originally either." Melissa adds.

"Okay, okay. I get your point. Points." Courtney grumbles, "There might be other people."

"Here's what I'm thinking. The food group can go off to see if we can find any other survivors. Our odds are probably a little better now that we've eaten a little. And with the lack of- of." Penelope hesitates before barreling on. "Anyway, our odds of getting around are better."

"So, what are we going to be looking for?" Neil asks.

"Really, I think we're just hoping to bump into other people," Brody says.

"We're just going to hope to bump into them? What about all the other 'people' we've bumped into?" Neil sneers, "We bumped into plenty of those."

"Shut it, Neil. Look, we know it's not the best idea to search the hotel-sized ship by ourselves, but it's better than just leaving them. Not helping when we can. Or not telling anyone about the situation." Penelope shakes her head, "We've gotta do something. It wouldn't be right to not do anything that might help."

... — -... ... — -... ... — -...

They're not as quiet this time. They're aware there aren't many infected, but they're also very, very aware they might get surprised if they're not careful about keeping an eye around them for anything or anyone that might sneak up on them.

Apparently, once Neil's halfway comfortable, it's impossible to shut him up again. Whatever magic Brody had used was apparently one use because it didn't work this time. "Oh man, it's gonna be great once we get back to shore. Only survivors of a cruise ship zombie apocalypse-"

Penelope couldn't help but flinch; she was trying so hard to avoid the word, even in her own head.

"-The press are going to be all over us. Everyone's going to want our stories-"

Neil was talking about how launching his 15 minutes of fame would be great.

"-Maybe we'll even be able to get book deals! Oh man, you know all the famous people who don't even write their own books? They have ghostwriters do it all, I bet-"

Penelope just wanted him to shut up.

She was sure all the others did, too.

He keeps going on, though, "-sure. It'll take a little bit of time, but I'm sure we'll be able to milk it for millions, and then we'll be living the easy life-"

And he was just uncaring of how many people had died, how badly hurt their friends, well, her friends, were.

It's just cruel and so small-minded.

He's so cruel and so small-minded.

"-Might even be able to turn it into a movie deal, then get on the big screen! Oh, can you imagine-"

Penelope struggles as he keeps talking, apparently keen on making up for everything he hasn't been allowed to say. She wasn't going to knock him out, as satisfying as it may sound, because they need him conscious. If he was unconscious, they'd have to lug him around.

"-Know, I always wanted to be an actor; unfortunately, you really just can't get work up here. I didn't want to leave my family in a lurch like that, so I didn't move. Vancouver's got a lot coming out of it-"

Which would only make this even more of a nightmare.

"-So if we can turn it into a movie, we'll be in anything we want to in a jiff, launch whatever careers we were hoping to-"

Still creeping along at a snail's pace, they hear fighting noises, half-words of zombies, and a woman grunting and yelling.

"-And the big screen would be good, but that's so flashy too. Maybe being a producer is more my style-"

"Shut up!" Penelope hisses, peeking around the corner.

Inside one of the rec rooms, a woman is fighting three zombies on her own. She's soaked in blood—a lot of it—and the infected she's fighting look fresh, barely more than the bite wounds they carry.

They watch the woman beating away the infected with a giant deck umbrella, which really seems like an unwieldy weapon, but she manages and manages admirably before pushing the infected off the deck by spearing them before opening the umbrella, which is badass and also terrifying.

Their whispered discussion follows the display.

"She just-"

"Yeah, yeah-"

"I mean, she looks fine-"

"*So fine.*"

"We could-"

"But is she safe?"

"We could ask-"

"She just killed *three*-"

"We need all the help we can get-"

"All that blood through-"

"What if she's infected?"

"I don't see any veins-"

"Doesn't mean they're not there-"

"We want her on our side, though."

"If she's infected, we're at more risk."

"We need her on our side."

"If she's infected through-"

"We'll leave her behind."

"We need the help, come on." Penelope pulls away from the others.

The woman pants, staring out into the water, apparently unable to hear them.

Penelope hopes she's not crazy. "Excuse me?"

The woman spins, lifting the umbrella up again but pausing when she sees them.

Penelope is uncomfortably aware of the woman's gaze raking over them, but she decides to push on: "My name's Penelope. This is Melissa, Brody, and Neil. We're looking for other survivors."

The woman slightly lowers her umbrella, "Sarah."

"Look, we're set up in the bridge, and we're trying to tell everyone left so we can get home," Penelope says, apparently their spokesperson now, "but we also need to make sure you're not infected."

"The easiest way is for you to show us." Neil pervs on her, but Brody shuts him up with an elbow to the ribs.

"You don't have to strip. Just tell us the truth." Penelope looks at the blood that's, well, covering her, "We're a little concerned, though. That's a lot of blood-"

"It's not mine!" Sarah insists, "It's not my blood, and I don't have any open wounds. I can prove it. I'll show you."

She starts taking her clothes off, but Penelope stops her.

Ignoring Neil's groan, she says, "You don't have to do that. We believe you."

Smiling gratefully at her, Sarah resettles her clothes, "How many others are there?"

"Well, we have eight people total; the other four aren't in any shape to be looking around right now, though."

"That's great, that's really great." She smiles. "What happened to the others?"

"Attacks mostly-" Penelope spots the way her hand tightens on the umbrella, "-None of them are infected. No black lines!"

Sarah looks at the others, checking their faces.

"We're looking for other survivors." Penelope asks her, drawing her attention again, "Do you know where any are? Or even where you think people might be hiding?"

Sarah pauses, "I think I know where a few are. I didn't try that hard to get into them. I didn't know if they were locked or had people inside. That and I didn't feel like getting my head beat in on accident."

"That's great! I mean, not the head-beating part, but would you be willing to show us where the rooms are?"

Sarah agrees.

25

Chapter 25

Sarah leads them to others, mostly individuals who'd bought food as gifts and survived off it, and they bring it back to the bridge. A few people still have some food left and are willing to share. They should have a little extra, and pooling resources is something they'll probably need to do to survive.

Penelope has the people they find pack a bag with whatever food they have left and as many blankets as they have available. They don't have any upstairs, and while it makes everyone bulky, it will be a lot better than just sitting on the floor all the time—and a lot better than just sitting on the dried blood and... other stuff caked onto the floor.

It was more than Penelope had ever expected to find, and she was glad about it. However, she was still worried about how many other people hid.

Everyone's anxious when they get back to the bridge. Henry looks more worried than she's ever seen him, Charlie's hanging out by one of the doors, and Courtney's resting in one of the chairs by Henry.

Penelope helps the others get settled first and foremost. All of them were horrified at the state of the bridge, blood caked to the floor, screens and windows smashed, and nothing but a few injured people standing guard.

But they all file in without much complaint, assessing and then acquiescing to the situation.

Once they're settled, though, Penelope can see the concern on everyone's faces.

It takes her a moment to realize she can't see Teagan.

It must be Teagan, who hadn't been in the best shape when they'd left but had been sleeping and looking a little better.

"What's going on? Is everyone okay? Is Teagan okay?" She can't help the questions bursting out as their core group reassembles, and Teagan isn't there.

"Teagan's okay," Henry's quick to soothe her, "In pain, but nothing that we should worry about now."

Brody's caught on as well, "Then what's wrong? Where's Teagan?"

"She's outside. There's— Well. Something's happened." Henry gestures to where Charlie stands by one of the doors.

Penelope rushes over, Charlie pulls the door open, and she's never been so glad to see Teagan.

Pulling the other girl into a hug, Penelope tries not to think about how she was sure Teagan had died or become one of those things.

"Whoa! What's going on?" Teagan says, not really fighting back against the hug.

"Are you okay?" Penelope asks.

Teagan wheezes and Penelope loosens her grip, "Except for my newly bruised ribs, yeah."

"Then what's Henry so worried about?" Penelope asks, looking Teagan over anyway.

"Those." While gesturing to the lower decks, Teagan says, "That's the problem."

Penelope looks down.

She wants to say something about hope, perseverance, and how they'll be okay, but no.

The problem is below them and obvious, even from the control deck.

The infected are swarming the decks. To Penelope, it looks like they're looking for a way off. But she's sure it can't be that. It can't be something quite so complex, so...

Rational.

It's gotta be something else like they're looking for food.

She wonders for a moment how likely it is that they will find other survivors. Maybe they could find the other survivors, with the infected racing around the edges.

"How did you..." Penelope almost can't fathom how close to death they got or how many infected were there with them.

"Find out?"

"Yeah."

"I got too hot, came outside to cool off a bit, and there they were." Teagan shakes her head, "We didn't know if you guys would make it back."

"We did, though." Penelope says, pulling Teagan into a side hug, being as careful as she can, "And we found other people, too."

Teagan nods, whatever noise she'd made lost to the wind.

Penelope can't take her eyes off the swarming infected.

More than slightly, it's unsettling how they circle the decks, all following each other and drawing more and more outside with their sounds. It's creepy and reminds her of those videos of ants circling around a phone or soda can.

And they're not falling off the ship like Penelope would have thought; they are just following each other around and around.

Before Penelope can ask, Teagan tells her, "I noticed them earlier, not long after you left the second time. Then, more of them started appearing after those ones. Maybe they heard something outside the ship and just started following each other after a while."

"Why," Penelope wonders, "Why do you think they don't attack each other?"

Teagan shrugs, saying, "I don't know, I mean, they do, I've seen it a few times. One of them triggers another, and they tumble to the ground together. Then, the other pile on, making it harder to tell. Sometimes, they get up again; most of the time, they don't. It's just harder to tell why they don't."

Penelope hesitates to ask Teagan to check over the new people. She's looking better, but it might be too much for her. And anyway, they're all saying they haven't been hurt, let alone infected.

"You found other survivors," Teagan says, nearly a question.

"We did."

"Did anyone check if they were injured? Infected?" She asks.

"No. They'd all locked themselves in."

"Someone should check them over." Teagan smiles, "Might as well make myself useful with all the laying around I've been doing."

26

Chapter 26

After getting checked out by Teagan, Sarah, and the other new survivors settle in to rest. They share the blankets they had, lucky that they'd thought to have those coming with them grab as many as they could carry. Thanks to that move, there's enough to go around. Along with the food, the group gets a bit of light air and a little hope.

Maybe it's a little easier to be hopeful when there are other people, and you have something halfway soft to lay on with food in your belly.

Penelope sits down herself, curled up near Henry, who's barely left the captain's chair, and offhandedly notices Melissa and Brody curling up together. It's sweet, but Penelope also knows they'll be insufferably trauma-bonded after this.

She didn't think she'd hate that, though. Brody had been a pretty good person to be in a disaster situation with, and he'd kept her friend safe this far. He seemed to care about her, and even now, they were talking about something making her smile. They were going to be good for each other, and she hoped she got to go to their wedding.

Neil, on the other hand, she hoped she'd never see again. Ever.

Even though everything is seemingly calm, Penelope can't sit for more than a few minutes. When she gets up, she first checks on Charlie, who's flipping through some manual he found earlier. This indicates a boredom level Penelope had reached a few times herself. Then Henry, who's also bored but dealing with it in the old man way by dozing off repeatedly. Courtney's on the radio, though she's watching the clock, waiting to call out again or to hear a response. There hadn't been anything since the other vessel told them they were on the way.

Teagan's resting now, for which Penelope is thankful. Her friend had been pushing herself too hard, even if she thought she was lying around. Fighting an infection on top of everything made it all the worse for her. At least they had food. It wouldn't last too long but would be long enough to stave off starvation for another couple of days.

Penelope still feels too wired to sleep or maybe too tired to sleep.

She couldn't even remember the last time she'd slept, but it felt like it might have been sometime last year.

Sleeping seemed impossible, though; she couldn't lay down to sleep.

A part of her brain was all too sure that if she did, she'd be plagued by the same kind of monsters that filled her waking hours. The time of sleeping was dark and heavy, and deep was gone now that there was something like safety and hope to be found.

It was better to stop thinking about it; she should keep watching or at least get some fresh air.

Penelope grabs something to eat before she settles in to keep watch on the swarm of infected below.

The can of peaches seemed so tiny but also so much. Still too careful about not making herself sick, Penelope barely takes more than an actual bite at a time. Even though her stomach clenches a bit even at that much food. Or maybe it's the lack of it.

It doesn't matter too much right now. She'd be fine if she didn't eat too much and make herself sick. She tries to focus on the moving bodies below.

The infected wander laps of the ship, and there are more and more of them when she looks away. They're acting oddly, too. She's not sure what she expects of them, but they really do remind her of ants. Granted, ants are much more likely to kill each other than others, but they are still ants. They won't be able to get off the ship without some course of action to get through the infected.

Time passes slowly, and even though they know it will be a while until the other ship comes to rescue them, Penelope's eyes still search the horizon, looking for anything that might be a sign of help on the way.

It takes her a moment to even be aware of it, of the fact she can see it. The skies have cleared because, of course, now they have, like a ray of hope, the rays of light are dipping below it. But they're there, they're still there. Sunset takes longer and less time than she'd thought before suddenly leaving the world in darkness and cold. The deck seemed colder now than it had when she'd come out.

Back inside, she's not the only one waiting less than patiently.

Courtney apparently refuses to leave the radio, and Charlie is camped out by her. Henry is very comfy in the captain's chair, watching the charts and data they show when he's awake. They're all just waiting for the other ship to signal that they're nearby, that it's time to move.

But there's just nothing.

They said it would take a while, but it's getting longer, later in the evening, in the night.

It seems like time is absolutely, boredly, stretching on.

Nothing is going on anywhere, really, no calls on the radio, no reaching shore, not even any stupid notifications of any kind on anything. No one's phones are connecting if they still have power.

Watching the ever-circling questioning of humanity waiting for a response and wondering what remains when you're gone is something to waste a little time, just for a little while, somehow better than doing nothing, but it only works for so long. Penelope joins Courtney and the kid, listening to the silence on the radio, but even that gets boring after a minute or so.

She takes action and scans the channels a few times, hoping for something. But there's nothing. Not even ideal chatter.

She scans the radio channels again and then again, hoping beyond hope that she'd just missed something, that something was going on, maybe some radio outage? She'd never heard of that before, but that didn't mean it couldn't happen. Right?

It's hard to rest in these conditions. She knows it is and knows that choosing to flip between all the different stations isn't helping anything and that she's making it harder for everyone else to sleep. But something won't let her rest, even though she's exhausted. More exhausted than she'd ever been in her life, even through the worst parts of exams when she'd been studying hours a day, sure this was the one she'd fail. It'd be the one that stood between her and the future she wanted.

She can't really rest, even with a complete lack of anything else to do.

It's too hard to even really settle down.

Harder than she'd ever thought it would be.

Harder than it ever should be.

But here she was.

She looks around at everyone, trying to figure out how they deal. Sarah is set up near the little map they'd been able to make work, along with Henry, Brody, and now Courtney; they're whispering. She can hear the jist of it, that they're kinda screwed unless someone shows up in the nick of time.

She's still putting her faith in the people who said they'd come for them. She has to hope they're really coming, that they're really going to help.

The other survivors are sleeping, which is not too surprising. Most of them had been on their own and with someone else keeping watch; they just crashed given the chance, except for Sarah and, apparently, Penelope.

She joins the others as they debate about sending a notification on the PA system.

"I just don't think it's a good idea," Sarah says, unsure.

Penelope listens to the conversation, letting the words wash over her as the others discuss, telling everyone there's a potential way off or to try getting somewhere safe before the ship inevitably crashes against the rocks.

"Guys," Penelope interrupts, "I'm not sure why there's a debate. Wouldn't it be better to tell them either way? They should at least know the ship is going to crash."

Sarah shakes her head, "I think, no, I know, the infected are triggered by sound. And if they're not, it's still one of the easy ways to get them riled up. If we do something with the PAs, it might rile up all the infected. Anyone not anywhere safe, or at least safe-ish, wouldn't be able to escape; they wouldn't be ready for it. We're just sending them a storm of hurt and death for something they could probably figure out on their own."

Brody shakes his head, "I think it's a risk worth taking."

"I agree," Melissa says next. "Most of the people still on the boat still think we're supposed to be landing in Vancouver tomorrow, I think. But they don't know that they're still at least days out."

"If they somehow still have food, or they're waiting until we're in port, they're going to be sorely disappointed and possibly die from starvation," Penelope adds.

"They should know," Charlie adds. "Right now, they don't know that it won't be safe if they're still hiding, or that we aren't going to be at shore tomorrow, that they'll die if they stayed hidden, that if they're in the front portion of the ship that they're going to die."

"Well, even if we wanted to find them, to help them, we don't have a clue where to start," Sarah says.

"That's a different problem." Penelope tells her, "But even if we don't know how to activate the PAs, or how to activate only some of them, we really, really, really needed to figure it out."

"And if we can't save them, then give them the best chance they could," Melissa says, a surprisingly mulish look on her face.

"It's something I think we need to figure out," Penelope says. "There's a chance we'll save our own lives if we can lure the infected away from parts of the ships we need to get to. And if we can warn anyone about what we're going to do, we might be able to save more lives."

"Wait, are you talking about using it as a lure?" Sarah asks.

"We know they follow the sound; why not this sound?" Penelope asks.

"It's worth investigating," Brody says.

"What if we could get other people out of the more dangerous areas by leading the infected away?" Henry asks, startling Penelip, who'd thought he was asleep again.

"Well, even better!" She says.

"Why didn't we think of this before going to the kitchen?" Neil whines.

"We actually didn't need it then. But we'll need it this time."

"So what do we do next?"

"Next, we figure out how it works."

27

Chapter 27

They take a moment to take stock of what they have, what they need, and what plan they have, if any.

"So what do we have?

"We have enough food for the time being, so we should have enough time to experiment with lots of things in the bridge, including the PA system."

"We have people now, a lot of them, it might be a little safer to travel in a group this way."

"Someone's coming to rescue us!" Charlie then adds, "Probably, at least."

"We have some medical supplies," Teagan adds, "it's not a ton, but it's something.

"I hate to be devil's advocate," Neil says next. Still, Penelope's sure that's just a cover, "We also don't know for sure if anyone's coming for us. The person might have said they were, but they haven't communicated since. We also don't know if the PA system works or if it's one of the things that has been destroyed. And we don't have enough food to hide until the ship crashes."

"I hate to agree," Penelope starts, "but yeah, we'll run out well before then."

"Teagan's hurt really bad too," Melissa continues, "Courtney too, being able to just rest helped, but it wasn't a perfect fix, and we're probably going to run through the medical supplies quickly with the shape they're in. We're already running out of bandages; we're just trying to keep mostly clean ones on them."

"We haven't really been covering Courtney's wounds. We didn't have any tape to keep something in place, and where they are, it would take pretty much all of it to keep her wounds covered."

"So maybe things weren't going as great as we thought," Sarah says.

Teagan shakes her head, suggesting, "We should radio out again. It's been a while since we heard from the other ship. Maybe they just got where we were going wrong."

"Unlikely, it's not like we've changed direction at all," Henry tells her.

"Well, it's only been a day-" Courtney says but gets cut off.

"It's still too long for my tastes," Neil says. We don't even know if the ship will reach us before the whole ship crashes."

"There's no use in waiting around then; we can, and should, reach out," Penelope says, her voice broking no argument. "Who's best with the radio?"

"I think I am," Courtney says, and it makes sense that she ended up with the most experience on the radio.

"Alright, get on the radio, try to contact whoever you got a hold of before." Penelope orders.

Courtney nods and starts trying to call out while the others figure out what they will do and what they want to fix if they can.

The others half listen to Courtney's calls to the void as they try to get the PA system working.

She calls out three times, but there's no response. Courtney tries again, immediately panicking, and the panic is evident in her voice, but again, there's no response.

The others also start to panic a little, and it's not just their core group.

Penelope can also see how it rattles the new people, who are all more fidgety and looking for something to do food, or something else.

She can't focus on that now, on the thoughts of the risk that these calls will go unanswered, too. Instead, she focuses on getting the PA to work. She tells herself it's not just for them but for the people stuck on the ship, but she knows on some level that that's not true.

A muffled squawk is how they know they at least got it on, a win in and of itself, a mini celebration just for that.

But then she hits a stopping block, "What do we say?"

The others look back at her as she looks around to see if anyone else has any ideas.

"What do we say?" Penelope asks again.

The old man doesn't know, simply shaking his head. Teagan is sleeping, and Courtney's suggestions are all terrible. She means well. They're just not good suggestions. Penelope finds her throat closing up when she tries to offer a suggestion.

Charlie ends up being the one to make an announcement.

He takes the mic, a deep breath, then starts. "Hello to anyone who might still be on the ship. We're in a bit of a rough situation. You've probably noticed the zombies, the infected, whatever you call them. They're dangerous, just in case you didn't know, don't confront them. Hide if you can.

"Listen, we're in danger, folks. The ship is on a course for land, and we're not going to be able to avoid it. We can't change directions or anything, and when it crashes, it will probably destroy the front of the ship, but you'll probably survive if you go to the back."

"Something else you should know, there's another ship on the way, hopefully, to rescue us. But I don't know when it's coming, if they'll be able to save anyone, or if they're tricking us into leaping into danger. We don't know yet and won't know until we actually get there. But here's the thing: we'll definitely not be safe if we stay here.

"So please, please get somewhere safe. Get to the back of the ship if you can. Just, stay alive, if you can. You're not alone; there are other people out there who have survived, too. But you have to try."

Charlie's voice breaks a little, and Penelope rests a hand on his shoulder, squeezing it, and smiles at him. Charlie's managed so well and kept his wits about him, something not everyone managed.

"Please, just try."

Penelope squeezes his shoulder again and moves to the windows to see if the infected would be attracted to the sounds.

The ones on deck swarm the speakers; she knows they can use it as a distraction.

But how long will it work?

At the moment, it's just a big, horrifying distraction while they wait for rescue or death or whatever else might come.

28

Chapter 28

"We gotta go!" Penelope's entire world feels rattled as hard as she's shaken awake by Charlie, who yells, "I'm on! It's time to go."

She doesn't remember falling asleep; she's tucked against the main computers, and someone has put blankets over her.

Fighting off the blankets, she can hear a voice over the radio repeating. "Attention Lady Lovebond. We are approaching your ship on the starboard side. We will match speed at the back of your vessel."

"Back of the vessel?" Penelope asks.

"We said we'd be there. I thought we'd have time to get there!" Courtney tells her, also rushing. "They said they're in sight of the ship."

"How long do we have then?"

"Well, if the ship is in their sight, then we've only got a few minutes."

Penelope looks around to see everyone rushing to gather what little they have, some slower than others. There's almost no question of carrying the food; it's not a conscious decision. Everyone's hungry, too aware of how long they'd gone without.

Some people take less time than others. Even from a dead sleep, Penelope is ready in minutes, though she's still blinking the sleep out of her eyes.

She slaps at the PA, trying to convey that there's help. Again, she falters.

This isn't the time, though; she's got to say something, "Hey! If you're out there, you gotta get to the back of the ship; another ship is going to meet us there, and if you're not there to meet them, they'll leave you behind."

Penelope uses her hairband to tie the PA on, even though they never figured out how to separate the speakers. She's about to leave, turning back to the others for a second, just long enough to see the scared looks, the fear, and also the determination, the will to live, and speaks to the PA, to the people who were still on the ship, those who still alive.

"Listen to me, if you're still alive, you're a survivor, even if you've been hiding in your room this whole time. You've made it this far. I'm not going to lie to you. There are some scary things outside your rooms. They might look like people, even people you know, but they're not anymore. They can and will hurt you, but you've got to try to survive anyway.

"Just try anyway. For you, your family back home, and anyone and everyone you've ever known that you want to see again. Try."

Penelope tightens the straps on her bag, makes sure the hair tie is secure, and leaves with the others.

... — -... ... — -... ... — -...

They've talked about getting around the bridge, going to the top to sneak past the infected, and going down one of the side ladders.

It wasn't a great option, but they might be able to get out that way.

Henry asked them not to. He wouldn't be able to get around, and getting down had been hard enough.

They hadn't gone that way, even though, looking back, it probably would have been faster.

Now, the group rushes along as fast as they can.

Henry is struggling with everything, trying to move fast. Still, it's obvious that he's having a hard time just walking without his walker, and fast is no longer a speed this man can.

Penelope calls the others, "Hold on, circle around Henry.

"It'll slow down the group, though," Neil argues.

He doesn't say it, and Penelope doesn't hear it; somehow, she can feel Neil suggesting they leave Henry behind. Even as they move to surround Henry, giving him support and moving fast, faster, fast enough that they won't miss the boat.

She won't say anything or even acknowledge the looks Neil is shooting everyone, trying to subtle signal it. Some of the others are looking back. No one's saying anything, but they're looking back.

Maybe they agree, maybe they don't.

Now isn't the time, not that it was ever the time, but they're already so close at this point, and she won't leave Henry to die just cause Neil thinks it would be easier.

Just because other people think it would be easier.

They're getting closer to the middle of the ship, where there's more blood, more of the infected, more chance of death, or worse. The time to sneak around was gone, and despite the group's efforts, this big of a group just couldn't be quiet.

It was only a matter of time before something discovered them.

Before noticing their group, the infected attacked one of the walls, likely trying to find whatever speaker the droning sound was coming from. A younger man, maybe about their age, rushes towards them with his mangled hands reaching for them, black veins crossing over them.

Sarah manages it quickly and efficiently, so swiftly that it takes Penelope a moment to realize what's happened.

Neil takes it as his cue to stop being subtle.

"Come on guys," He's whining, an irritating high pitch, "We need to move faster. We shouldn't wait for him. He's going to get us killed!"

"Shut up!" Penelope hisses, "We're not leaving *anyone* behind!"

She could go for the low-hanging fruit, the fact that he can't go much faster than the old man, but she didn't believe they were going to die waiting for this old man.

"You're going to get us all killed! Survival of the fittest!" Neil's voice rises in volume again despite the others hissing at him to be quiet. "We just gotta run for it!"

Penelope yells at him, "Shut up!"

It at least shuts him up for a moment. She knows it will probably bring unwanted attention their way, though.

They'll try to find an alternate route to get them out of there.

"We need another route; we're too exposed," Penelope says. Look for a map or something."

They don't split up; everyone looks butstays close to the others.

"There's a map of the ship up here," Brody says, pointing off to the side,

"Great. We need to get to a section that has less of the infected," Penelope says as they crowd around the map, looking for where they're supposed to be and where they need to go.

Neil's dropped, leaving the old man behind for the moment. The routes he chooses, though, will be harder for him.

"It will be nearly impossible; at least, the speakers seem to be drawing them away. Maybe not away from other spaces, but it'll at least give us a little space to move as long as they don't notice us." Penelope tells the others.

"We should just go down the main halls," one of the other survivors says. It's not like we have time for guesswork here."

"She's right," Henry says, "Our time is limited at best, and if we hesitate, it'll be gone."

"It's not impossible, with as large as our group is," Melissa says, "As long as it's not too overloaded with infected, we should be able to get through."

"There's the chance we might lose someone or multiple someones." The whine was back. "If we go along the outside like we did earlier, it'll probably be safer."

"Now's the time to think about that and even consider it an option." Penelope says to the rest of the group, "We've got to focus on just getting out of here; if we try to choose the perfect route, we'll never leave."

"The decks outside have to be safer, though," Neil whines again.

"If we had more time, maybe we don't, though," Brody says, an uncommonly severe look on his face.

"Main hallway it is," Penelope says, turning down the path they'll have to take.

They hurry along; it's not that far, and they are only literally on the other side of the ship. It is practically the furthest point they could be trying to reach. It'll all be okay if their group keeps moving forward and doing good, good enough.

The infected they'd bumped into wasn't the only one.

More of them appear, slowing down the group.

Even injured, Brody and Penelope take up the front against them. With Teagan's IV pole, Penelope shoves them off to either side, at least out of the way for the others to pass or deal with. They don't have enough time to deal with them appropriately. They can't afford to stop, turn back, or find a different route because it's too late to signal to the other ship. If they waste too much time, the other vessel won't be able to help them if they're not there to meet them.

They're too close to fail, too close to getting off this godforsaken ship to stop, to risk getting stuck here.

Penelope pushes them off course, remembering a couple ladders that go almost all the way down to sea level. She'd noticed them on the ship in one of the ports; maybe they could help now.

They won't be all the way at the back, but it'll be close enough for the other ship to see them and come around.

And if the other ship doesn't see them, maybe they'll think they've died.

Leave them there for whatever fate comes to them.

No time to think like that, no time to hesitate. They need to get to the back of the ship, the ladders, and soon.

"Where are we going?" Teagan is the first to ask.

"Outside of the ship, there's an area where we'll be able to climb down a ladder, maybe even get close enough to the other vessel to safely get on it," Penelope tells her, aware, so very, very aware that they're going to an area where there was a lot of the infected earlier.

"Lead the way," Henry says.

Penelope looks at him, sees how exhausted he, Charlie, and all of them are, and fights for her second wind. Just trying to keep the others alive would have to be enough for now.

There are more infected people than they could have thought or realized. There are just so many of them all the time.

There are too many, and they just need to get past them.

The other survivors aren't very well armed, and they're not trying to kill the infected; they're just trying to get them out of the way, at least enough to pass.

Teagan, Charlie, and Henry are at the center of the group. Though they're still pretty adept at knocking infected themselves, Penelope barely sees the old man's fist flying up to knock away a would-be attacker she hadn't noticed.

A door behind them blows open, and the area is overrun, a million times worse than before. The speakers still work; she can hear them. Why didn't they keep distracting the infected?

They knock out a few, knock over a few, and try to keep moving; they're limping. The sheer numbers are nearly too much. They have to keep trying; there's no other option.

It's fighting or death, survival or infection.

Penelope throws off the woman that'd come right at her, though it takes her IV pole with it, and sees Neil is struggling face to face with another infected. It's stronger than him even though it's half his size and pushing closer, half words dropping from its lips. It's too close. He will probably bite his face if it or he gets any closer together.

Penelope doesn't think. She just grabs the closest thing that could be a weapon and knocks the zombie in the head with a shuffleboard weight.

She doesn't even know how she noticed it.

It wouldn't kill the zombie, but it's better than nothing.

She slams the weight into its head again, trying to get it off balance.

And it does; it knocks the zombie off balance.

It knocks Neil off balance, too.

There should be a life vessel at that section, but now it's an opening to dead air.

Neil's eyes widen, and he's no longer struggling against the infected but gravity; he pushes against the zombie, pushing to get both of them back to safety.

But it doesn't work.

They slip off the deck to the inky waves below.

Penelope dives to the edge, trying to see where they landed, but the ship is moving too fast, and any cries are covered up.

She calls out, but he's already gone.

Courtney tugs her up, blood rushing through her ears.

She can't hear anything.

Looking down, looking over the edge even as Courtney drags her away.

A slap centers her, and she looks back to Courtney. She can't hear the other woman is words over the rush in her ears, but she gets the gist: They have to keep going.

They have to. Most of the zombies are gone or down, but those remaining are already rising.

She didn't mean to kill him, as annoying as he was.

She's gasping, suddenly not enough air in her lungs.

They can't stop, can't go back, can't look for him.

She keeps the weight as a weapon; it's pretty good at knocking the infected away.

She didn't mean to kill him.

They have to move forward; they have to keep fighting.

Brody's hurt; he keeps looking back, and his friend is gone.

Penelope keeps to herself that she's not exactly upset that Neil's dead.

She'll take it to her grave.

29

Chapter 29

Somehow.

Somehow, they fight their way through the swarm.

Penelope was there. She knew how they did it, but she couldn't make it make sense in her mind. One second, they were fighting for their lives, then she was looking for Neil, and then they were hurrying along to the next place, the next room.

A little battered, a lot scratched up, down one person, but somehow that was it.

They'd only lost Neil.

Back inside, they sneak past another group of infected and down a staircase to one of the lower decks, one of the areas that's small and probably cheaper but still has a window out of the ship.

Going over the railing to get to this ladder might have been easier.

But there was no way Henry could climb down multiple floors on a ladder, and Teagan probably wouldn't be able to either.

It takes more effort to bust out the window than they'd thought, a lot more, actually, and it won't be an easy squeeze-out, but it's close to the ladder on the outside of the ship. They'd at least be able to get down that, get low, instead of just jumping into the water and hoping for the best.

The number of infected that they've tossed is—she doesn't even want to think about what might be close to the ship. Even at the speed they've been going, it's probably surrounded by things waiting for a treat.

Penelope isn't a confident swimmer and never has been.

She didn't even like being fully submerged in water, and she didn't know if an old man or kid would be okay or if they'd need help swimming.

Doesn't know if Teagan can swim or how many others can.

No, it's better to just be able to go to the other ship.

The window is tough, but not tough enough to survive the onslaught they put on it to get out of the ship. They're so close, so so close to being able to get out of here.

They toss a couple of blankets through the window, partly to help protect themselves from the sharp glass still there and to flag where it is, where they are really. And it's immediately soaked from the water outside. Saltwater pelts down onto the floor through the tiny window.

Penelope hopes that the vessel on its way to meet them will be able to see where to get them. They'll just have to do it, get through, and get onto the other vessel.

A few of the survivors lean out intermittently to look for the ship and avoid the infected, who occasionally push each other off the ship. It seems like there are more of them dropping down than before, and it's worse when they notice someone is below them, as multiple of them will fall off at a time.

How will they be able to get down the ladder without being taken out by falling infected?

The infected have to run out eventually, don't they?

Don't they?

Melissa is the one to notice a much smaller vessel approaching them and keeps time with them. She tells the others that their rescue is here, at least that she hopes it is. It might be the right ship, but it might not be.

Others look. It had to be the right ship. If nothing else, it's a way off of here. It's holding back, probably trying to figure out what to do with all the infected milling around on the upper decks.

Shouting and waving probably isn't the best bet, but they don't really have another option. It'll alert the infected above and, hopefully, the ship below, too.

The ship draws closer, but it's still too far away. They know it's time to start the climb.

One of the women they'd rescued climbed down first, so fast she was like a cat, down and jumping across like it was nothing like she'd done it every day of her life.

More of the other people go, including Charlie, and manage to get across. Some land softer than others.

But the zombies have noticed what's happening below and start falling at increasing intervals.

Watching the others climb down and jump at the right time to land is nerve-wracking. Even though they go down as quickly as possible, it's hard to get down when the infected keep falling around them, grabbing at anything and everything they can.

Brody climbs out first, shuffling as close to the far edge of the ladder as he can before calling for Henry to get out,

Henry may say he doesn't need help, but given his struggles and his exhaustion from the rush, they all know he's going to need some help.

Melissa and Brody both help as much as they can, Brody from below and Melissa from above or beside him.

It's a struggle to get him down safely; his joints don't bend, and Brody can only support so much of his weight along with his own, and he doesn't feel that he can jump to get across.

It's a far fall, and given how much he struggles on flat land or a flattish ocean, getting him jumping will be an issue.

Watching from the window, Penelope understands; she really does, but if he doesn't make it, they're all screwed and stuck on the cruise. Somehow, they get him across, and he rolls. Seeing him roll is terrifying; she's sure he's going to be hurt, badly even, yet it looks like he avoids anything worse than bruising, somehow.

Penelope was sure he'd break something, but magically, no.

Melissa jumps right after him, too much right after him, trying to catch the same swell that'd lifted the smaller vessel for him, but it drops from beneath her.

She breaks her leg, the snap of it audible even from up in the room, her shriek drawing more of the infected off the ship.

More survivors follow, trying to get across as quickly as possible but more carefully after that. It's not easy, and one of the other men gets dragged into the water with a Z, gone before they can move to help him.

Penelope doesn't think about how he'd sunk quickly, lost to the waves before they realized he was gone.

Not the time, not the time. Penelope doesn't look back while she climbs down, doesn't look up, looks where she's putting her feet and hands. When the smaller ship is rising, she jumps and makes it across.

Though she's sure, she sprained her wrist.

Not the time.

She cradles her hand and watches the rest follow.

Everyone else ends up with bumps, bruises, and a couple more sprains, but somehow, they all make it.

Penelope would be crying from joy if she wasn't so shocked.

One of the men on the deck, whom she hadn't noticed before, asks if anyone else is coming out of that room, and a chorus of no's answers back.

They're pretty sure they're it.

They'd hoped, they'd waited.

The man gestures to the one driving.

The infected keep falling all around them, and too many hit the boat on the way down for comfort.

They have to move.

The smaller ship peels away, leaving the cruise on its dead straight course.

...— —... ...— —... ...— —...

The whole group is left on the open front of the ship.

There really isn't enough to cover all of them. They're pelted with salt water, but it smells fresh and clean, and Penelope has never been more glad to be alive. Only a little longer, and they'll be home, only a little longer, and they'll be able to put this all behind them.

The smaller ship practically flies across the water, away from the coast and the boat that's been their prison, away from the horrors they'd endured.

Penelope can't help but watch the cruise ship disappear.

It's been a nightmare, worse than a nightmare. But it was finally over.

Just a little longer, just a little further.

She'd lost her phone a long time ago, but maybe someone would let her borrow theirs to call her mom.

Land—she hadn't realized they were so close—is to their left, and they're flying by it, but her eyes stay on the ship. She's pretty sure that means they're headed south.

She hadn't realized just how close they'd been.

How long until the ship crashed?

Not long at all, but at least they weren't on it.

At least they'd warned whoever was left behind.

... — — ... ... — — ... ... — — ...

Later, much later, when the cruise ship is out of sight and has been for a long time, Penelope refocuses on the group, really looking at them.

Someone's tied Melissa's leg into a splint. It's barely there and doesn't look like it's holding the bones in place, but it's probably the best they can do.

Teagan, Henry, and Charlie are tucked into the small covered area. Courtney and Brody are tucked as close to the others as possible. They're not covered but are still sharing body heat. All of their wounds have fresh bandages, most of them sloppily done but better than they were before. None of them look good, but they look so alive.

They look like there's a chance for them to live. They look happy, and Penelope hopes they'll be okay when they get home.

It should only be a matter of time till they get to shore, Penelope thinks, or to wherever they'll be docking. But they're not heading toward shore; they're heading toward a cargo ship with other smaller boats around it, all rocking in the waves.

The closer they get, the more Penelope notices.

About a dozen smaller vessels are tied to the ship or floating strangely close.

It seems like odd behavior.

Why would they all be tying up to the other vessel? Why not go to shore?

She can't ask, though. All of the crew of this vessel are obviously doing their jobs as the smaller vessel goes around to the other side and ties up to the much larger one.

Armed people stand at the edge of the larger vessel, watching as they approach. The crew guides them back to the center of the deck, but they won't explain why so many people with guns are already there.

Penelope trades looks with the others, but there's no escape now.

They don't have any weapons, and they're all too injured to put up much of a fight anyway.

More people with guns and proper weapons arrive, and any fight Penelope has is gone. A million worries and fears run through her. But they're surrounded by people who could kill them in an instant, who stand over them as they're crowded toward the cargo ship.

They have no choice but to climb to the larger ship's deck.

The group is kept under gunpoint as they're led to an empty container. At least it's safe, and there's no blood or body parts. Or even dried blood. It's actually relatively clean, a little dusty, but cleaner than anywhere they've been in days and miles, and it's better than anywhere they've been in the last week. However, there's still something odd about it, something wrong.

And then the doors are closed.

One of the gunmen, well, one of the armed fishermen, standing guard, says it's for their safety, to keep them out of the way.

It doesn't feel right to Penelope; they're being imprisoned.

Like they're being held captive for a crime they're not even aware of.

Minutes pass, then hours.

They settle in as much as they can, huddling together and putting the more injured people further to the back. They've got to protect their own, and they don't know what will come next.

Finally, the door opens again, revealing a tall, severe-looking man in hip waders and a dark beanie. He looks them over slowly, observing each person before he waves away the guard. Penelope looks right back at him, trying to memorize the scars dotting his face, the much deeper one that barely misses his eye cutting along the right side of his face.

She doesn't know what'll happen next, but she's ready to face it head-on.

"I'm Captain David Roberts." The man introduces himself, voice calm and commanding. His voice is a rich, deep baritone that surprises

Penelope. "How much do you know about what's happened?"

The End...

For Now

About the Author

Ellowyn Beimler is an author living and writing in Southeast Alaska. When she's not at work she spends most of her time reading, gaming with friends, and exploring the beautiful island she calls home.

If you happen to find a typo in this book (or you really liked something) email Ellowyn at Ellowyn@nerdworthy.com

You can connect with me on:

🔗 https://ellowynbeimler.carrd.co